Pride Publishing books by Bailey Bradford

Single Books
Breaking the Devil
Dark Nights and Headlights
Texas and Tarantulas
Belt Buckles and Cowboy Boots
Something Shattered
Yes, Forever
The Jasper Soul

Southwestern Shifters
Rescued
Relentless
Reckless
Rendered
Resilience
Reverence
Revolution
Revenge
Reluctance
Renounced
Retrograde

Southern Spirits
A Subtle Breeze
When the Dead Speak
All of the Voices
Wait Until Dawn
Aftermath
What Remains
Ascension
Whirlwind

Love in Xxchange
Rory's Last Chance
Miles To Go
Bend
What Matters Most
Ex's and O's

A Bit of Me
A Bit of You
In My Arms Tonight
Where There's a Will
My Heart to Keep

Leopard's Spots

Levi
Oscar
Timothy
Isaiah
Gilbert
Esau
Sullivan
Wesley
Nischal
Justice
Sabin
Cliff

Calendar Men

Mr. January
Mr. February
Mr. March
Mr. April
Mr. May
Mr. June
Mr. July
Mr. August
Mr September
Mr. October
Mr. November
Mr. December
The 13th Month

Coyote's Call

Off Course
In from the Cold
Blue Moon Rising

Mossy Glenn Ranch
Chaps and Hope
Ropes and Dreams
Saddles and Memories
Fences and Freedom
Riding and Regrets
Broncs and Bullies
Hay and Heartbreak
Vaqueros and Vigilance

The Vamp for Me
My Life Without Garlic
Don't Stake My Life on It
Sunshine is Overrated
Don't Drink the Holy Water
The Trouble with Mirrors
That's One Cross Vamp

Spotless
Hide
Hunt
Home
Heart

Mystic Tattoos
One Too Many

Valen's Pack
Run with the Moon
Exodus

Power
Exchange
Submit
Dominate

City Shifters
Bearly There
Harey Situation

Wild Ones
Destined Prey
Destined Predator

Mossy Glenn Ranch
Chaps and Hope
Ropes and Dreams
Saddles and Memories
Fences and Freedom
Riding and Regrets
Broncs and Bullies
Hay and Heartbreak
Vaqueros and Vigilance

Fire & Flutter
Dragon Dreams and Fairy Wings
Wyvern Ways and Elven Magic

Anthologies
What's his Passion?: Unexpected Places
What's his Passion?: Unexpected Moments
Racing Hearts: The Lonely Ones

Fire & Flutter

WYVERN WAYS AND ELVEN MAGIC

BAILEY BRADFORD

Wyvern Ways and Elven Magic
ISBN # 978-1-83943-984-1

Interior text design by Claire Siemaszkiewicz
Pride Publishing

Published in 2020 by Pride Publishing, United Kingdom.

Pride Publishing is an imprint of Totally Entwined Group Limited.

WYVERN WAYS & ELVEN MAGIC

Dedication

To whoever needs to hear this—
don't quit before the miracle.

Chapter One

"Ow!" Brick grabbed at the hand slapping his face and glared at its owner. If he hadn't known who was hitting him, the selection of bright cocktail rings and the jingling bracelets she wore would have told him it was his younger sister, Scarlet. "Any reason you're smacking my face?"

Scarlet tilted her head, her forehead creased. "Habit? Whatevs. Hold still—"

Brick held still enough for her to shove wads of cotton wool up his nostrils, then brushed her hand away. Scarlet's sharp fingernails near any of his body parts made him uneasy at the best of times, and in the rumbling, jolting carriage he and she were currently traveling in, more so. Her nails were long and pointed and they gleamed the brightest mahogany shade she could find, all to mimic the talons they became when she shifted.

Well, that's only natural, Brick reasoned. Wyverns in general were proud of being wyverns, the ruling family even more so and his sister, the youngest offspring of the Ruby Throne, in particular.

"Thanks," he muttered, the thick clog in his voice not just due to his nosebleed and the wedges of cotton wool. "Thanks for staying with me." He knew she'd rather be flying alongside the carriage with their father, Potentate Carnell of the Ruby Throne, and mother, the First Lady Cerise, not to mention the son and heir, Lord Gules, and their older sister, Lady Vermillion. But it was her turn to keep him company, and Scarlet, like all of them, put family duty first.

"Sit up straight," she replied, wagging a finger in the direction of his face to tell him it was the best way to deal with a nosebleed. She knew. All his family did—Brick got them when he was around magic, and they were prepared for today. "Open wide for your pills."

Brick obediently opened his mouth, and Scarlet, snickering, moved back to the farthest corner of the royal carriage and flicked in first one tablet, then another, using her middle finger and thumb to launch them as if she were playing a game and getting points. Scarlet performed her family obligations, sure…and made sure she had fun doing so. But she loved Brick, just as he did her.

He tried not to choke—the tablets were huge and foul-tasting. "Thanks," he repeated, wishing she'd thought to give him a drink to swallow them down with. Actually, no—he didn't want her squirting it in with a water pistol. He checked the cotton wool was still in place up each nostril. "There must be a lot of magic in the air here."

"Well, duh," his sister replied. "Inside the elven kingdom, and just approaching the capital? What d'you expect? They breathe it in and fart it out here, then breathe it in again." Oh, she was a charmer. "I got orders to smarten you up—you're not gonna bleed on me, are you?"

He shook his head and let her pull his smart suit jacket into place as if he were a baby, for all she was younger than he was. *Well, that fits, with me being as useless as a hatchling.* She tutted and brushed off the shoulders and lapels, as if he had flaking head scales. *I don't, do I?* That'd be all he needed, with them having to look their best as they arrived for this regal state occasion.

As soon as Scarlet settled back again, grumbling that there wasn't much she could do with his short hair, he took a sly peep in the glass of the carriage window to check for scale-flake. He caught a quick glimpse of his bronze skin and slitted gold eyes before the spectacle outside claimed his attention. Oh, not the well-maintained kingdom they were driving through, with its paved roads, sturdy-looking buildings and general cleanliness all signs of its good governance, but his family, in the air above the small procession.

Brick lowered the glass to see better. The four royal wyverns made a stunning, vibrant swoop of color as they flew, their wings beating with synchronized grace, their heads turning slowly on their long, elegant necks to incline this way and that at the gasps and applause from townsfolk lining the route, who were all eager to see visiting nobles and dignitaries.

"Elven folk must be used to flying beasts, right?" he asked Scarlet.

She scoffed. "Not like us."

"Yeah." Brick had to admit that. A woman stumbled, shading her eyes against the wyverns' shimmering scales, the gleaming shades of red carefully arranged from his father Carnell's shining cardinal to his mother Cerise's glossy pomegranate—"*the first seen in the kingdom in a hundred years!*" as she often reminded people.

His brother Gules' proud imperial red came next, then his sister Vermillion's brash crimson. The family at wing, in the correct order, looked like flames burning up the sky.

Although why they should want to arrive anywhere making the place look like it was on fire, Brick couldn't fathom. What he did know was Scarlet wanted to be up there too, making an entrance like a bold streak of lava against the blue and white of the sky. He jumped as the most jewel-colored creature of the quartet swooped low and stuck her beak through the window—his mother, checking in on him.

She couldn't talk in her shifted form, of course, but he had no problem interpreting her caw and twists and jerks of her head. She was concerned for him—she loved him. They all did. *Like they would any slow-witted hatchling.* He wasn't wily or cunning, no asset in statecraft or trade negotiations, so they gave him busy work. *Grunt work.* He nodded to show Cerise he was fine and reached up to pat her on the head, near the top, just after the brow ridge finished.

With a click of her beak, she took off again and rejoined Carnell, circling him with a slow flap of her wings before taking her place at his side. He flicked his tail out to slide along hers.

"Oh, *ewww*!" Scarlet, on the seat opposite him now, pointed up at the Potentate and First Lady and retched like a caterwaul bringing up a hairball. She made a show of rummaging for one of the sick bags they kept for Brick—there was no telling what form his sensitivity to magic might take. "Old people foreplay is just *gross*."

Brick didn't think it was that bad. Sure, he had no wish *whatsoever* to see his parents making out like subadults or immatures *ever, anywhere,* but that they were still loving and affectionate was...something he didn't see himself ever having. The only people who'd wanted him so far had been those seeking a way into the ruling family and using him as their way to get within polishing distance of the Ruby Throne.

"Mommy, look!" A little girl on the sidewalk near a tavern, her eyes full of wonder, tugged at her mother's arm. "Up there—dragons!"

"*Wyverns!*" yelled Scarlet, flinging herself so far out of the window to correct the kid that Brick, alarmed for her safety, grabbed at the back of her dress. "Look at the picture, small fry!" She tapped the crest on the side of the royal coach, a plain outline of an almost S-shaped beast, its wings stretched and its slim legs prominent. "Count the limbs, kid. There's two, not four. We look like lumbering oxen dragons to you?"

She subsided into her seat again and shot Brick a glance. "No offense, bro."

"I know." Brick was wide and tall, built like a brick smokehouse, as the saying went, whereas wyverns, in addition to being wily, were light and lithe. Winged serpents, really. He tried not to feel like he was letting down the Ruby Throne, but...

"*You're not even red!*" Olahf had scorned when, realizing a relationship with Brick wouldn't bring him into the inner governing circle, he'd ended things between them. "*Brick by name and brick by nature and brick by color!*" Yeah, Olahf didn't really have the gift of eloquence a senator or diplomat should, although his tongue could be said to have been silver in other ways… Brick shivered at the memory, then felt sad.

How much of that had been fake? Had Olahf even liked him? If not, their relationship had been, well, transactional at best and *icky* at worst. It had also made him dwell on his experiences with all the other wyvern shifters who'd befriended him over the years…and hadn't seemed very friendly. How many had if not used him, then put up with him, for what they could get out of it?

Would life have been different if I were called Flame, or, or Rosso? Maybe if the former, he'd have been dashing and just a *little* bit dangerous, or if the latter, darkly seductive and a lot more dangerous?

"Persimmon's a good name," he mused out loud. "Then Sim would be a good nick. 'Hey, Sim, coming out for a quick tankard of sack mead?' Maybe Simmy? 'Simmy, joining us for dawn patrol?' Perse? Percy?"

"What? No—you know what? Never mind." Scarlet waved a hand at him. "Because we're nearly there."

About to ask his sister how she knew they were almost at their destination—where they'd be doing some trade-and-aid diplomacy over drinks—Brick saw the ceremonial herald bird flying to join the four wyverns in the sky. The escort would please his mother, who was into appearances. Even his father had commented more than once that the elves had used to do things properly, and that he hoped the Storm King was keeping up traditions.

"He will as long as he has Jerrick advising him," Cerise always replied. *"Jerrick served Jade's father, too, and Jerrick's father, Jacron, was chancellor to the Storm Emperor before that. And Jerrick's son—"* She usually stopped herself there.

"Gotta love ya and leave ya!" Scarlet opened the carriage door even though the vehicle was still trundling along.

"I feel okay now the meds have kicked in," Brick assured her. "Shouldn't I join in?"

"And risk you having an allergy—sorry, *sensitivity*—attack up above and bleeding down on Jade or his big green groom?" Scarlet sniggered. "While it would be hilarious, best not." Blowing a kiss over her shoulder at him, she launched herself from the open door.

Scarlet shifted effortlessly in midair and took her place just behind Gules and Vermillion. It was hardly worth her shifting, though, when the carriage jolted to a stop at the top of a meadow. Two ruby and pale jade pavilions stood proudly, their pennants waving in the early evening breeze, and councilors and nobles waited before them.

The Ruby Throne circled the meadow in a group, then made a tighter circle of the tents to finally drop into the space set up beneath the main pavilion's awning. They descended one at a time from Carnell to Scarlet—all executing flawless landings and simultaneous shifts back to their other-forms the second their claws touched the ground, clothing themselves as they did so.

They'd left a space for him, and Brick decided he was going to take it properly, instead of scuttling to it, shamefaced. Ignoring his headache and throbbing nose, he ran a few paces and leaped as high as he could with a gurgled "*Eaaarrgghhh!*" to shift into his wyvern form and, oh, how good it felt to be in the air again, stretching his wings.

He liked the world better in his shifted form. He loved the view from up on high, how things looked when seen from his bigger, more golden than yellow eyes. Scents were more acute to his snout, with its slits for nostrils, than to his other-form nose, which was broad and had never worked as well after being broken during a heated game of tail ball. Which his team had still lost.

Okay, so he wasn't all polished and gleaming reds like the others, but he liked his scales, with their rust and terra-cotta and ochre shades. Recalling Cerise's insistence that his hues were "*alternative reds*" made him snort with laughter and swish his tail, the triangular barb it ended in swinging near his face.

He was going to do this! He dropped lower. *I can do this! Can drop into that landing zone!* The really small landing zone… *I can't do this.*

"*Believe in yourself!*" Cerise had told him over and over since hatchhood. He would. He did! With a high-pitched squeal, a bit like a teakettle coming to the boil, he took a final squint at the target zone, landed, shifted and…belched. *Oh gods.* He'd meant to clothe himself, not burp one out. And certainly not such a loud one…or one that stank like a dragon's taint.

"Oh, *ewwwwwwww*!" cried Scarlet, her longest ever. She pinched her nose closed with her talon-like fingers. She'd get the worst of the stench, being next to him. "How, *how*, is that so foul? What the fuck you been doing, bro, sucking off a troll?"

"Could have been worse!" called a voice from the crowd. "Just imagine if he'd farted!"

Chapter Two

Jagger glanced up at the palace servant whose cock he had down his throat, trying to decide if he looked more scandalized now than he had a few minutes ago.

The blond page—Steven? No. That didn't sound... *Ah, Stephan, right*—had worn shock like a part of his livery on seeing Jagger earlier, and not just at Jagger, the royal-adjacent elf, being in the palace library. Although that would have been understandable enough. A place of scholarly learning and intellectual study wasn't Jagger's natural habitat.

And as if the sight of *Jagger, Jagger, sword and swagger* among dusty, sneeze-inducing tomes hadn't been enough, Stephan's eyes had widened, and his mouth had gaped farther when Jagger had reached out and looped a hand around his neck to bring him in for a kiss.

Stephan's astonishment had turned into bewilderment when Jagger had pulled him into this small storeroom tucked into an alcove—perhaps the page knew Jagger didn't do that well in confined spaces?—and his expression had slid back to scandalized at Jagger slipping off his sword belt and sinking to his knees in front of him. According to royal protocol or palace hierarchy, it should be the page servicing Jagger—a councilor and son of the chancellor—and not Jagger giving a lowly servant a blow job.

"*Sir!*" Stephan squeaked as Jagger, holding eye contact, firmed his hard palate and sucked. He'd wager no one had taken the blond page this deep before, or slurped quite so filthily, or tickled the bundle of nerves under the head of his dick with the tip of his tongue like Jagger was. Elves were one of the few species that were more sexually promiscuous than Love fairies, and Jagger was probably the most uninhibited in all the court.

Humming, he swiped his tongue over every vein and wrinkle of Stephan's dick, relishing each whimper and pant he pulled from him, and loving how the page snatched his tasseled livery cap from his head and shoved it into his mouth to muffle his squeals and cries.

A second later, the page stamped a foot on the floor, telling Jagger he was feeling the cool tingle around his cock and balls. *Just a tiny bit of herb lore.* Not a keen student, Jagger knew the basics of elven magic, like shimmers and glamours, and enough earth craft to…enhance things. To spice things up. In this case, a smidgeon of contact magic to make his mouth feel like the coolest freshest peppermint and—

"*Ahhhh!*" Stephan spat out his cap and bit down on his hand instead to gag himself.

And the slyest, wickedest hint of hot cinnamon. Enough to make Stephan give a final buck of his hips and shoot his load down Jagger's throat in record time. Jagger swallowed Stephan's cum and pulled off slowly, licking the page's cock clean as he did so. He liked giving head and was good at it, and Stephan tasted great. Jagger bestowed one of his crooked smiles on him as he got to his feet.

"Sir, you…you didn't…" The servant's face glowed a bright red even in the gloom of the drab closet.

"You mean I haven't. Not yet. I will when I fuck you, in about thirty seconds," *Jagger, Jagger, tongue and dagger* answered. He reached out a finger to tip up the page's chin, needing to see his face to assess what state he was in. *Only a little fucked-out.* Sex with Jagger could make some of the lesser elves totally blissed-out, or give them a fuck-high, as he thought of it—a by-product of elven magic.

Stephan's eyes were wide again as Jagger one-handedly popped the buttons on his tight leather breeches. He used the other hand to strip the page's stupid uniform pants off him, at the same time yanking off those ridiculous shiny shoes that Jade liked the household servants to wear—for a joke, Jagger assumed.

There was no need to remove his own trousers, only peel back the placket. They fit his legs like a second skin and allowed him freedom of movement *and* looked amazing with his knee-high boots. He backed the page against the shelves lining one wall of the closet. Stephan stumbled against the high, wide ladder Jagger had barely noticed leaning against the shelves, but that he studied now.

Interesting. Assessing possibilities, Jagger crowded Stephan, pushing himself between his legs and shoving at his feet until, floundering, the small page had to step onto the ladder's bottom rung to right himself…and raise himself to the height Jagger wanted. Stephan flung up his hands to grip the ladder's sides, level with his head, steadying himself, and Jagger admired the picture this made.

He regretted not having time to nuzzle and lick, suck and nip. He liked exploring a partner, learning all their hills and hollows, where they liked to be stroked...and bitten. He tended to leave his mark. Abs and pecs were his thing. Well, his upper body thing—there was plenty on the lower body he liked to get his teeth into. And that being the case, Stephan might as well keep his double-breasted little-drummer-boy jacket on—the slender page didn't have much torso terrain for Jagger to explore.

He had sweet slim legs though, and Jagger enjoyed running his hands up their outsides, then back down the insides, feeling the softness and suppleness. He smirked to see that Stephan's spent cock, shrunk to acorn size after his massive climax, was trying its best to stir, wanting to get in on the action. Jagger gave it a swift lick, to be going on with. "Sit," he ordered, and Stephan, when he'd caught on, sat gingerly on a rung.

"Slide forward. Sit back."

Stephan didn't get Jagger's impatient and unclear instructions, so Jagger pulled his ass forward and tilted his chest back for him on the slanted ladder, making the page bend his knees to use the rung his butt sat on as a footrest too. It looked lewd and dirty but didn't expose his ass enough for Jagger's liking. Wrapping his legs around Jagger's waist did, though. "Better."

Stephan's knuckles tightened on the sides of the ladder when Jagger stroked his ass cheeks, admiring their pertness, and Jagger tutted. "I haven't even touched you yet," he griped, giving Stephan that few second's warning before he grabbed and squeezed, learning the texture and testing the resilience of his partner's ass. Stephan bit back a moan, some of it escaping when Jagger touched a finger to his hole. *Tight.* He loved screwing a guy after he'd come, when his muscles were still contracted from his climax. But he'd relax his partner first.

Jagger felt in the hip pocket of his leather jerkin for the small pot of balm in there. He unscrewed the wooden tub one-handed and scooped out a dollop. He was used to the slightly sour smell of the unguent but wondered if Stephan would react—he was following every movement Jagger made, almost unblinking.

"Is that…?" he whispered.

"Just tagmallow." Jagger understood the question. "Thick, but just simple lubricant." *Nothing aphrodisiac.* He wouldn't use something like that, like the fluid from peruinan flowers or—gods!—huzz orchid honeydew, without discussion. He didn't need to, not if the way Stephan bit his lip and his fingers tightened to the point of desperation on Jagger when Jagger circled his hole with a lubed finger was any indication.

The page's first ring of muscles gave way and Jagger teased his finger round the whorls guarding the entrance, then eased in. A noise outside the door had Stephan jerking his head in that direction. "*S-sir!*" he hissed, freezing and clamping down on Jagger's finger.

Yeah, this was crazy. Anyone could come in and find them, Stephan pantless and Jagger with his pants open and his hard, erect dick wanting in to Stephan's ass, and no way to deny he was about to screw the page's brains out.

"Want me to stop?" Jagger offered, pulling his finger almost out but continuing his slow swirl that was softening Stephan's hole to accept—and crave—something a lot bigger. When a quiet "No," came in answer, Jagger grinned. He eased back a little to coat himself in the lube then made sure Stephan's legs were wound tight around his waist, forcing him flush against Jagger's body…with the head of Jagger's dick pressing against his hole.

He caught his partner's gasp in his mouth and breathed, "Ready?" against his lips. Before Stephan could reply, could even nod, Jagger thrust forward, pushing the head of his cock just inside him, letting him get used to the thickness and stretch. He held still for long seconds then pushed a little more, a little farther, the tight heat that gripped his cock making him throw his head back and grunt.

His head in that position made him notice the long, narrow strip of mirror on the back of the door and he cast a quick look at himself. The sight of his opened leather jerkin and billowing white shirt, his tangles of curly shoulder-length hair made him forget the closed, narrow, low-ceiling room. He thrust deeper, making Stephan grip tighter to both the ladder and around Jagger's waist, rocking with the hard, fast pace Jagger set.

Ideally, he'd have fucked the page until his moans filled every corner of the closet and he was ready to come a second time. Then Jagger would have wrapped his hand round Stephan's on his filling-again cock, working it until it engorged, the head glistening as it emerged from the grip of their joined hands. But this session, all he could do was make sure he rubbed over that gland inside his partner that had him crying and weak, then thrust harder and deeper one last time, to shudder in a quick but satisfying climax, one that had the both of them groaning.

Jagger pulled out of Stephan's ass slowly, enjoying the ripple of its muscles along his dick as he did so. The page's arms trembled as he let go of the ladder's sides and he shook his hands to get the blood flowing there again. Jagger helped him unwind his legs from his waist and set his feet on the floor. A glance around showed him a soft cloth, no doubt used for wiping book jackets, and he snagged it and passed it over. "Here. Clean up."

Stephan tried, looking dazed. *Wrecked.* "Will I…?" He made an effort to raise his averted gaze. "Will I see you again?" he got out in a gabbled rush.

"Sure. We both work here," Jagger replied, tucking himself in and buttoning up.

"I mean—" The page pressed his lips together almost as tightly as he had when trying not to scream a few minutes ago. Which seemed to remind him to look for his hat. When he retrieved it from under the bottom shelf, it looked rather the worse for wear.

Jagger took it and tapped it on his knee, glamouring it a little, and handed it back.

"Thank you." Stephan had a sweet little smile. It was what had attracted Jagger's attention yesterday. Well, that and his equally sweet ass. "Sir…Jagger. Will we—?"

"Sure. Why not." Jagger meant it. He could always use a palace snack, a morsel on hand to complement the smorgasbord he enjoyed in the town, at the tavern. He had his own room there—it had once been Jade's. Before Grlind, of course. *Lucky Grlind. Lucky Jade.* Well, good thing for Jagger that the palace servants rotated. He'd have been bored stupid else.

"But even with the prophecy?"

A bell tolled before Jagger could ask the page what he meant.

"Daemons' horns." Jagger scowled. "I have to help prep the Great Hall for dinner later this evening." Not that he intended to do much but taking on that task meant he was excused all today's last-minute council tedium, most of it meeting and greeting delegations and trying not to yawn while he did so. Thank the stars no senior councilor had tried to force him into *that.* They all tended to be lenient and indulgent with Jagger, with him having lost his mother at a young age—well, young by how long elves lived.

His father, Jerrick, was still recovering from her death—their mate-bond had been so strong he would never think of taking another. The custom was to choose again from the same family. Although Tahly's family had paraded forward various cousins and nieces over the years, and a couple of her old friends who'd remained unbonded or become widowed had offered themselves—or more recently, their daughters—too, Jerrick remained loyal to Tahly's memory.

Jagger knew how much his father still grieved and how lonely he'd been for many years now. He was determined not to go through any of that and avoided a mate-bond. *Prison sentence, more like. Never mind the agony and sorrow of losing them, what about the mind-numbing, soul-extinguishing monotony of having sex with the same person? Every. Single. Day. Ugggh.*

"Sir, the prophe—"

"Not now." Jagger shushed the page. Whatever he was babbling on about—and Jagger had no idea—could wait.

He buckled on his sword belt then ran his hands through his hair to settle it and blew a kiss to his companion before making his way out of the closet, glad to be free of the confined space.

His sword swung at his side and his boot heels rang on the stone floors as he strode the corridors and halls to the Great Hall, casting the tiniest bit of a charm to make sure he looked clean and fresh when he entered.

Chapter Three

The laughter that greeted his loud, noxious belch and the witticism someone had called out in response made Brick wish he could sink through the ground like it was a yurt bog. The flurry of apologies—his to his parents, his family's to their hosts and fellow guests—and the rush to clothe him was mortifying. He wanted to slink away into the small crowd as soon as he could and wondered how he could make himself look thinner and shorter and generally more elf-like, to blend in and lose himself, but knew it wouldn't work.

It wasn't possible, anyway, because it was his duty to be part of the wyvern group. Well, to be on his own in the wyvern group. He took a deep breath and tried to make his face smile and wear a look of interest at the proceedings. He was curious and liked seeing and learning new things. He was happy to be here for the wedding of Jade, the Storm King, and his chosen, Grlind. It was just that his efforts tended to go wrong, and usually sooner rather than later.

With effusive, "Your Excellencies!" the councilors and courtiers were immediately crowding them, their greetings fulsome and long-winded. Brick looked longingly toward the bigger tent, where the chink of glasses and plates meant the food was. He'd much prefer grabbing a trencher of food and a tankard of malt ale or wheat beer—or whatever the local brew was—at the tavern he'd passed along the road. He cast a glance back the way he'd come. It couldn't be *that* far...

As if knowing his younger, gauche brother was contemplating bolting, Gules sidled up to him and spoke with his hand covering his mouth. He tended to be over-cautious at any public event like this...and it tended to mean a reprimand was coming. "Mother says can you at least *try* to look as though you want to be here?"

"I *am* trying," Brick protested. "This is my 'interested in the new place and its people and customs' look." He forced himself to stop eyeing the top of the field, where the road was. The route would probably lead him to the palace anyway, and more of this bowing and scraping. Ha—there was *literally* a quartet of musicians bowing and scraping away at their wooden instruments on a small platform to his left. Would his brother appreciate the joke?

"And Father says keep your eyes peeled and your ears to the ground," Vermilion edged over to them to add.

Brick wanted to give a Scarlet-like, "*Ewwww,*" at that. His eyes watered at the thought of being peeled. "Not literally?" he asked, fingering an ear and pointing at the lush grass.

Milly gave her patented older-sister-to-a-fuck-up-of-a-little-brother sigh. "Brick, wyverns are—"

"Wily. Yeah, I know."

"And the Ruby Throne is only as secure as—"

"Its underpinnings. I know that too. Like I know we're all on show. That all this is for show."

A nice one, however. The elves had put on a dignified welcome, with the tents that were a clever blend of Ruby Throne and Storm King colors set up for the use of the family and their retinue. Servitors in Storm Palace livery waited in twos and threes to spring into action and the scent of citronella, to keep away whatever bugs this kingdom had, competed with the sweet smell of pale lallit flowers set in tall vases on half-pillars. The effect was tasteful and a flattering compliment—those blooms were Cerise's favorite.

Brick caught one uniformed servant gazing at him, but supposed the guy was checking out his slitted pupils rather than his face or bod. People did stare at his strange-looking eyes, so much so that Brick sometimes liked to wear dark glasses in new places, among new people.

"Where's Sylph?" he thought to ask. Their family's—well, the Ruby Throne's—air elemental servant was mostly invisible, but Brick could usually detect its presence, even before it manifested with its customary shimmer. "Keeping away from the fountain?"

Sylph would avoid even this ornamental, contrived contraption that was splashing out sparkling water and wine to drink. Brick stuck a finger under the drops and licked it. It tasted fine to him, but their elemental didn't like any type of water, even a trickle of the stuff.

Gules studied Brick. "If you're lonely, why didn't you bring someone? I know you aren't...*with* anyone," he added before Brick could speak, "but there's room in the second carriage—you could have invited a friend?"

Brick sniggered, thinking of his drinking bro Flad at an event like this. The guy had no patience for anything of this nature and no pretensions either. When he'd met the First Lady, it had been when Cerise was congratulating the guards who'd just graduated from training and asking them what was next for them. Flad had replied, *"I'm gonna stay drunk for a month."* And when Cerise, blinking in bemusement, had explained that she referred to his future plans, Flad had said, *"Yeah, so did I,"* and winked.

He'd also called her by her original name, not the one she'd taken on marrying into the Ruby Throne, which had enraged her to the point her face had burned red. Brick had stopped Flad commenting on how well *that* fitted in with the ruling family color scheme.

But yeah, he did wish he had someone. Gules was betrothed to his soul-bonded, Marija —who already had Magenta picked out as her marrying-in name—and Vermillion was happy with her current pair, Krystle and Hans, whom she had no intention of settling down with...well, not for more than a few hours at a time, anyway. He imagined walking around a celebration like this, or any of the stuff planned for the royal wedding, arm-in-arm with someone he loved and who loved him.

Someone I can laugh with too. And go drinking with. And who likes all this diplomacy and ruling stuff. Who's handsome, likes sex and preferably has a big d—

"Does it mean anything that Jerrick, the Chancellor, isn't here yet? Or that his son isn't expected at all?" Carnell swung by to hiss at them out of the side of his mouth, covering his action by holding a silver cup to the splash of the fountain, to fill it.

"Jurgen's high up, and so's Jodhi. Over there, look. You can tell by their names how royal-adjacent they are," said Cerise, on his arm.

"Hmm." Carnell seemed placated.

Brick wouldn't expect Jade, the Storm King, to be here at some meet-and-greet like this, even if everyone was coming to the kingdom for his wedding. He must be far too busy with the preparations for the ceremony, as would his mate, Grlind. Brick studied the massive portraits of the couple that were hanging from the big pavilion.

Jade, the Storm King, the leader of the Elves, stared back regally from his painting, the tips of his pointed ears visible through his long black hair, the markings on his forehead clear. There was no portrait of Jade, the Storm Queen—there'd be no point, Brick supposed. The royal blood made the Storm King able to switch genders, but the face didn't change, just the body attached to it.

Grlind was, well, an orc. Literally. Brick wasn't name-calling. His race meant that the guy shone the color of fresh peas, the shade now known as Grlind green, Cerise had told them. He was bald, and his head sort of lumpy…a bit like a dish of mushed peas, in fact.

"Ewww," muttered Scarlet, seeing where Brick was looking. "Like, *really* ewwww."

"Don't let anyone hear you say that," her mother snapped. "You know we're here not just as fellow rulers from a neighboring realm to celebrate a royal wedding, but also to strengthen ties and revive old alliances between our kingdoms."

"Bet the 'happy couple' is too," Scarlet deadpanned.

Brick wasn't so sure. All he saw was the love shining in both sets of eyes, elf and orc. He wanted that. Yeah, he was lonely.

"So we're all here to do what's expected of us. Every one of us." Cerise looked first at her daughter then at her youngest son.

Brick shrugged. "Not much I can do," he admitted. He wished there were.

"I wouldn't be too sure of that," replied his mother, and the steel in her gaze softened a little as she eyed him. For a moment, a sly and almost calculating look crossed her face. "No, I wouldn't at all..." She walked away to the larger tent.

What was that about? Brick opened his mouth to ask Scarlet, but she turned and mumbled something, making a hasty escape. *Huh.* Brick didn't know what was going on, didn't see how he could help out his family...but he knew he didn't like the feeling settling over him. The breeze wasn't cold, but he shivered nonetheless.

His heart heavy, Brick plodded after his sister to where they'd be eating local refreshments. He hated these things but he knew his duty. This pointy-topped tent was large and everyone stood chatting around high tables, which saved working out the protocol of who could sit before whom. *Always a nightmare.* As were the dainty little chairs people seemed to favor for these diplomatic occasions...and that Brick always seemed to crush to matchwood or get his rump stuck in.

Cerise accepted a tiny cup from a bowing servant, dug out what looked like a glowing cherry with her little finger and licked it into her mouth. She downed the drink then threw the cup into her mouth too.

"Really?" Brick muttered. His mother should know. "Okay... *Ooh.*" The drink was sickly sweet and the small square cup was made of chokolaite, he discovered. Crunching it made him miss what the just arrived-elderly man, the chancellor, was saying. Something about his son being too busy with something but joining them later.

Cerise seemed to know the man. Herrick, wasn't it? *Jerrick, right.* Brick helped himself to a second tiny cup and listened to his family walking that fine line between being social and showing off.

"Gules just got his wyvern breath now he's bonded, yes." His proud momma beamed. "And it's a peacemaking, tranquilizing ability!"

"Useful when his little lady kicks off, eh!" joked an elderly council member, his shining row of service medals proclaiming his senior rank.

"Useful in diplomacy, yes. And it's the exact opposite of his father's," Cerise added.

Carnell had gotten storm breath, making him powerful, which was more useful in negotiations. Brick's sigh—not wyvern breath, because he couldn't ever see himself finding his soul-bond and so gaining that special wyvern power—ruffled a pile of napkins, making a servant grab them.

He thought he'd better take himself off and slipped into a quiet corner, out of everyone's way. He was no use in a situation like this, just as he had no value in making alliances or treaties or anything that would benefit his family.

"Not true. The prophecy?" A glimmer then a gleam and Sylph was there, picking thoughts out of Brick's head as usual.

"What?" Brick's neck ridges wanted to rise, and he wasn't in shifted form.

"The prophecy that says the wyverns will help the elven kingdom and the elves aid the wyverns too."

"That's…nice?" Brick didn't like the jagged glints Sylph was giving off.

"Good, because it's through you."

"*Me?* I hardly think so."

"I know so. You're coming to live here."

Sylph must be moon-addled. "I'm what now?"

"You'll be living here when you marry one of the Storm King's royal-adjacent councilors, fulfilling the alleged prophecy, but really as collateral for the mutual aid alliance." Sylph glittered diamond bright and steel hard.

"Counc…" Brick stared at the group, all of whom were wrinkled and wizened like—

"Trolls' nutsacs? I think you picturing trolls' private parts is something your lady mother should know about." Sylph vanished, probably to tell her.

"Come back here!" Brick cried. "So I can tie you to the ceiling and spin you around and use you as a disco ball! What…? Why—? The hell?"

He was to be given over, as if he were mere goods from their land, like a jar of gymph wine or a wrap of ged curd cheese? He staggered from the tent, making for the fresh air. *Arriving* in the elf kingdom had made him unwell, but knowing he wouldn't be leaving? That had put him under a death sentence.

Chapter Four

Whishhh! The ax flew through the air of the Hall. *Tunnng!* It landed in the barrel of beer on its stand beyond the far end of the long wooden table.

"Wait for it," Mikel, the palace's Great Hall steward and ax thrower, advised the eager onlookers, and sure enough, seconds later, the barrel split with a *creeeak* and, to loud cheers, the drink flowed from it. The guests stamped their feet in approval and the pages catching the stream of ale in goblets and passing them out were smiling.

"I hereby declare the first wedding celebration banquet open!" Mikel yelled, to louder applause. He lifted his cup and took the first swig, as he should, to test it was fit to drink—and not going to poison the Storm King—then held it aloft to signal that everyone could and should follow suit.

Not that they need any encouraging, down this end of the Great Hall. Jagger, one of the few councilors or officials there at the moment, took a cup and had a healthy gulp too. These long tables with their fixed benches were for the lower ranks. Jade and Grlind, when they arrived, would be in the thrones up there on the raised dais, not down here behind the open fire.

"Think it's going to work?" he asked Mikel. "This more informal first feast plan?"

Mikel shrugged his vast upper body, slopping his beer, and gestured at the townsfolk who were marveling at the Great Hall's vaulted ceiling and ouro-thread hanging tapestries. It hadn't been his idea to ask the lowliest of the kingdom to arrive well before the highest, but he had to make the best of it. "Maybe. Yeah, the staggered invitations probably *will* make this lot feel they've rubbed elbows with their betters but be finished and out so they're not gawking at them for too long while they eat."

He would probably be too conscious of his place—and Jagger's—in the hierarchy to ask if it had been his or the chancellor's idea. Jagger couldn't have cared less about who ate when and didn't think the plan had come from his father. *The chamberlain probably.* He hadn't been paying enough attention in all those boring planning meetings to recall. He wandered about, nodding at people he knew from the town—well, mostly male elves he knew from the tavern.

A couple of them gaped in amazement to see him here like this, one of the first in the Great Hall, his mahogany curls washed and bouncing, and him resplendent in his newest leather breeches. He'd polished his boots and sword. He had a dress uniform of course, and he'd wear it—if forced to—at the actual ceremony but not before. It had a triangular hat with a long, curled feather on it, that he wouldn't put on his head for all the gold in the vaults, if he had his way. The last time he'd had to don the outfit, the stupid feather had bobbed around his face and tickled his nose and chin. He'd been *that* close to plucking the ridiculous thing off and turning it into a pen.

And virtue was its own reward, as they said—being here early got him first look…and first pick. There must be some possibilities among the arrivals. Weren't the cabal of mages, from the seminary beyond the Crosswise Mountains, arriving today? He'd love to see if the rumors about what exactly the seminary's curriculum consisted of were correct. The things mages were reputed to be able to do…

Jagger peered around the hall but couldn't see any tall figures in deep indigo cloaks. There were only elves, arriving in droves now. That was the actual name for a group of them. Well, an adult group—the collective noun for young elves was a mischief. In his case, fitting. And hey, he *was* young!

"Son!" Jerrick beckoned him over, looking flustered. "You've been circulating down there, yes, as I suggested? And anything to report? Any new faces? Anyone stand out to you?"

"Huh?" Jagger pulled his wrist from Jerrick's shaky grip on it. "Dad, I don't need you prying into my affairs! I can find my own…entertainment, shall we say. And I'm sorry I have no intention of finding the one who stands out, or however you put it, but—"

"What? Son—" Jerrick glanced around and nudged Jagger behind a pillar. "I'm not referring to your…to anything like that. I meant the threats! Haven't you been paying attention? Did you at least read the minutes of today's meeting?"

Of course not. About to say, 'What do *you* think, Dad?' Jagger realized how serious and even flustered his father was. "Remind me?"

Jerrick tsked. "That not everyone is happy that the Storm King has chosen to marry someone outside his own kind! Some people are against interspecies mating. And not just people here, in the elf kingdom. Prejudice is universal."

"Hatred, you mean. Bigotry." Jagger paused. He'd heard murmurs, in the Cock and Balls, the local tavern where he spent most of his free time, but not actual conversation. Hust, the landlord, had a very strictly enforced *no politics, no religion* rule. "But there's been nothing concrete?"

"There've been protests!" Jerrick wiped his forehead with a linen square. "You know how careful we had to be in choosing the routes the guests took through the town to the palace, to avoid certain areas. Certain neighborhoods. We've had to use a little magic to shield the processions from anyone not wishing the visitors well, those without joy in their hearts for the union." He replaced his handkerchief in his pocket and accepted the cup of water Jagger took from a page's tray for him.

"I have to admit, I never knew it was possible," he admitted, waving a hand at the enormous portraits above the thrones. "Bonding, between different species."

"Talking of different species, the ogres are late," Joziah inched up to tell them. He lifted the seal on his chain of office. Bespelled, it changed into whatever the chamberlain might happen to need at any given time, and it was currently a big fat gold watch with a clear face and a loud tick.

"Oh, they can't tell the time and no page wants to go to their rooms to call them!" Jodhi, the chief steward, wheezed at his own joke.

"Oh, not their fault…that they couldn't read the itinerary!" Hareth replied.

Jagger expected the senior councilor to slap his thigh after that rib-tickler. "What were you just saying about prejudice, Father?" he asked, raising an eyebrow.

His father, who'd been chortling a little at the pathetic jokes, had the grace to look ashamed. "Come. Let's take our places," he suggested, sweeping his fellow councilors along to their section of the table on the dais.

It was situated under the Councilors' Gallery of portraits hanging on the wall, and as always when he was in the Great Hall, Jagger noted the resemblances between Jerrick and the painting of *his* father, Jacron. Grandfather Jacron had been chancellor too, the most trusted and loved advisor to the Storm Emperor, Jade's parent. Jagger supposed Jerrick's portrait would hang there too when he left the earth. Would they remove Jacron's, then? And Jagger would sit where his father was now? *Gods.* The hall they were in was big enough, but Jagger felt it closing in on him.

Nah. I'm unlikely to make chancellor. It had to skip a generation at some point, even if their family had always served the high court. *Through famines and feasts, insurrections and celebrations…* He couldn't remember the rest of the family creed and wasn't that cut up about it. It didn't even rhyme anyway. *Or scan.* He switched his focus to the servitors laying out their wares with practiced, swift movements.

The Great Hall was filling up before his eyes, the different groups entering to fanfare and polite ripples of applause with the fancier or more exotic guests provoking the occasional gasp. One group coming in the east door had everyone about them craning their necks to see.

"The Ruby Throne," Jodhi leaned over to tell Jagger. "You'd be interested, hey?"

Why would I? Jodhi turned to the person on the other side of him before Jagger could ask him. He didn't care much, anyway. The noise rose if not to the ceiling, then to the minstrel galleries on either side of the room. A trio of musicians was making their way to one, weaving their way through the streams of nobles, courtiers and burghers.

Jerrick had hardly sat before he tsked and stood, hurrying to the thrones to align them better. Jagger couldn't see any difference when his father had finished and doubted the Storm King would either.

The place stilled, then everyone rose to their feet and broke into applause—Jade and Grlind had entered the hall. Jade, switched to his female form as the Storm Queen, waved the guests to their seats again, and the pages bustled up and down once more. Palace guards ringed the room, standing discreetly against the walls, and Jagger now understood why. Threats, his father had said. Why, for gods' sake? All the Storm Queen had done was choose to be with the person she loved. Even if that brought no advantages to the kingdom. *Even if it brings the opposite.*

Jade suddenly looked at him and beckoned. Jagger considered pulling a *'who me?'* act and looking behind him but got to his feet and approached the thrones. He gave a low bow.

"Your place is here with us." Jade, now in male form, indicated the first chair that wasn't a throne at this top table, to his left.

"It's my honor," Jagger responded, and sat. Did Jade have him confused with someone else? Unlikely—they knew each other. *Oh, wait.* Was he supposed to be delivering some speech or announcing something? He really should have paid attention in the meetings. Well, whatever it was, he'd pick up enough cues to wing it. He usually did. He took a huge gulp of litch wine in preparation.

"Mister Jagger..."

Jagger almost jumped. Grlind hadn't spoken to him yet this evening but was now bending around Jade's back to do so. "Sir?"

"Just Grlind. Look, the Storm King choosing an orc means you all gotta work hard at making better alliances to defend the kingdom against attacks from outside, right?"

Jagger knew that. Everyone was always on edge about trolls and ogres possibly joining forces, for instance. He gazed over at the latter. He hated ogres. As if sensing his thoughts, one stared back at him and made a cutthroat gesture. *Charming. Not.*

"Right?" Grlind repeated.

"Right. And, of course, I'll do my best to help."

"That's real sweet o'ya to take it like that." Grlind's face stretched into a big green smile.

"It?"

"The prophecy, that says ya gotta marry one of the wyverns to cement their alliance with us!" The clap Grlind landed on Jagger's shoulder nearly had him on the floor. "That's what Jade's announcing now, to start the wedding celebrations off with," he continued, leaping up to pull out Jade's chair for him, because Jade was getting to his feet.

"What?"

Jerrick stood, and Jagger tried but failed to interpret the look on his father's face. "But…" he tried again, and anything he might have said was lost in the Storm King's proclamation about a wyvern-royal adjacent pact, one that might have been saving the kingdom, but that was effectively ruining Jagger's life.

Chapter Five

"Sylph, I said I'm sorry!" Brick apologized again, but nevertheless threw the remaining contents of the bucket over the air elemental. "At least it's warm water, right?"

He was genuinely regretful that he'd tricked Sylph into his room and flung half a bucket of water over it. No—he was sorry that he'd had to do it. But if he hadn't, hadn't ensured that Sylph was too weak to dematerialize, the elemental would have vanished from his room and gone straight to Cerise. For all his mother had married into the Ruby Throne, she was its head, its momager, and as soon as Cerise had joined the family, Sylph had begun reporting to her and doing her bidding.

Brick rushed into the adjoining bathroom and soaked a towel in water, again making sure it was warm. He wrung it out until it wasn't dripping, then retraced his steps into the bedroom and placed the towel over Sylph, as if he were covering a loquil bird in its cage, tricking it into stopping talking. "Sorry," he whispered, opening his door quietly and sneaking out.

Brick was doing more than creeping out of his room—he was leaving the palace. And he wasn't just slipping out to clear his head—he was, well, running away. He'd been speechless after learning the fate his family had planned for him. More so, when Scarlet had let slip the arranged marriage was being announced that evening, and he had faked a bad headache to get out of the feast and to be left alone in his room.

Sylph had taken his place in the Great Hall—literally, taking on his essence to embody him. The replication was temporary and basic, something like a solid image, but it would have appeared Brick was present among the Ruby Throne. *And they're all about appearances, aren't they?* His thoughts were bitter.

Moving slowly, a result of wearing two sets of clothes as a means of carrying a spare outfit with him, he crept down the smaller, more rudimentary stone stairs from the tower, the flight used by servants. *Fitting, as that's all I am to them.* No, that wasn't fair. He loved them, just as they did him, and he should do his family duty. Well, he would.

He might not be intending to perform the task they'd mapped out for him, and he was leaving his home, but he could still work for them, like a roving ambassador or diplomat, creating goodwill and trade and deals from afar…once he'd learned how to. From however far his new life took him. *And who knows, on my travels, I might meet someone…*

Fine, so he had no doubt he'd mess that up, as well, like he did everything, but it was still better than being handed to some old man as a bribe. A guarantee. Or whatever they wanted to call it. Funny, he'd never have thought his mother was a pimp, but… "You think you know someone," he muttered, trying to feel better in the dark and on the twisty steps.

Oh, thank the gods, he'd reached the bottom. He made his way along the short passage, guessing from the noise and scents he was near the kitchens. His stomach roared. He'd skipped dinner. Maybe he could take a little something to be going on with. And something for the journey. And breakfast. Before the thought had finished forming, he'd grabbed a big rectangular basket from a pile on the floor, hefted it onto his shoulder to hide his face and hip-bumped open the swing doors to the kitchens.

"How dare you come in here!" yelled a man in an apron, swinging a ladle at him as soon as he set foot inside. "With that? All refuse and waste is taken out of the kitchens to the midden by the blue door, there! How many more times do you lack-wits need telling?"

"Not their fault, Claune." Another apron-wearing man patted the first's shoulder, thankfully not with the hand that was holding a sharp knife. "The townsfolk we had to take on while the place is so full just don't understand fancy palace ways."

"What, fancy palace habits like not mixing food and trash?" yelled Claune.

"But the basket's empty," Brick replied, his voice rising from its usual baritone to end in a squeak when he thought about disguising it halfway through.

"Then fill it and take it out!" Claune screeched, stamping a foot.

Hunched over, Brick followed the man's pointing finger to the far wall and a huge vat of vegetable peelings, eggshells and scraps. He copied another helper in dipping his basket in and scooping some up, then scuttling outside. Through the blue door. On his way, he snatched at what he hoped were apfels…only to discover they were onions. *Oh, minotaurs' horns!* He couldn't even steal food right. Despondent, he headed off, turned back to dump his basket of waste then set off again.

At least he'd gotten out of the palace. Now all he had to do was shift and work out where he was by the light of the moon, so he could fly out of this kingdom and start a new life. Right, he'd just shift and— He couldn't shift. No matter how much he tried.

"Oh, pixies' foreskins!" he whimpered, clutching his head that felt as though an iron band was tightening around it. "What—?"

Magic. He'd forgotten about all the magic sprinkled around this place. This *palace*. Well, he was a wyvern shifter, for fuck's sake! A big tough *royal* wyvern shifter who could power through and—

"*Gahh!* Sorry!" he apologized to the night for the tremendous fart he'd let rip and that was even more stagnant-marsh scented than his belch of earlier.

He rummaged in his pocket for his meds, and his fingers closed around the onion he'd pilfered. Maybe that was stopping him? Why had he kept it, anyhow? He threw it into the air and drop-kicked it away. "Ooh, sorry!" he apologized again, this time to whatever creature of the night he'd hit and that screeched its pain. "I'm not normally a good shot."

Yeah, that'll soothe its feelings, Brick shithouse, he berated himself. With his luck, the animal was a treasured pet of some royal menagerie, who'd go rushing back to inform on him. Brick raced for the front of the palace and the route he'd come in by earlier. He'd simply retrace his steps until he was out of magic range, then shift and start the next Chapter of his life. What could go wrong?

He got lost. "It looks different in the dark!" he whined to no one in particular, stumbling. Why did it have to be such a cloudy night? Suddenly, as if granting his wish, the moon eased out from behind its cover of clouds. Brick exulted. There was enough light for him to see a meadow. Oh, it was where they'd had luncheon, earlier! It felt like days ago.

He trudged on and came to a crossroads he thought he remembered. The main part of the town was probably that way, and the kingdom gates *that* way. Unless it was the other way round. He turned, so he was facing the same direction he had been when he'd arrived this way earlier, but that didn't make things much clearer.

If his family were looking for him, daylight would make it easier to find him, particularly if he were wandering round in circles. What he needed was someone who knew the lay of the land and also knew a shorter and quicker way out of the elf lands. An elf guide, in short. And he knew where to find one—that tavern he'd glimpsed down that way! A new spring in his step, he hurried off into the more populated streets.

Two women were leaning against a low wall at the end of a paved street. Brick cudgelled his brains to recall the name of the inn. *Oh yes.* "Excuse me, I'm looking for the Cock," he asked.

"No cock here, just pussy," replied the older-looking one, with a lick of her lips. She studied him. "Ooh, wish I was the Storm King—I'd change for *you*."

"Leave off, Cameth," the younger one said. "It's just down there, see. Follow the music. Yeah, you'll find what you're looking for there, hunk."

Brick wondered if she were psychic. All that magic about in the air here must be doing something to people. "Thanks!" He set off.

"Tell Hust that Hayling sent ya," she called after him.

Hust. Hayling sent me. Brick repeated the names and instruction to fix them in his head and obediently followed the sound of fiddles and the thump of drums, to arrive at the wooden tavern. Two-storied, it was bigger than he'd remembered from the quick glance he'd gotten from the carriage earlier. A spicy meat and gravy aroma sneaked its way out of the open windows, making Brick's mouth water, and a sour beer smell escaped when a man stumbled out through the doors to stagger into the street.

The drunken man knocked over the free-standing board that advertised today's fare, and Brick helped the man to his feet, then righted the sign. Jackalope pie in spelt-wheat-beer gravy was today's dish. Even the *words* looked delicious. The colorful drawing of the fruit platter the place also served caught his eye too. But he wasn't here to fill his stomach. He pushed open the doors and went in.

The music was being made by a group of musicians in the middle of the room, and Brick went to join the people standing there, stamping their feet and clapping in time to the jolly tune. An elderly couple were dancing, spinning each other around faster than their age would have suggested possible. Brick applauded them and joined in the cheering and whistling for the music-makers when the song finished.

He weaved his way to the long bar counter. "Hust?" he called, when the noise died down enough for him to make himself heard.

A broad-shouldered man, his plaited beard grayer than his long hair, looked up, a goblet in one hand and a cloth in the other. "Yeah?"

"Hello. I, erm, I'm looking for an elf. Someone who knows his way around, to show me. I'm new here. Oh, Hayling sent me," Brick finished in a rush.

"Hayling? Say no more." Hust tapped his nose. "Up the stairs, first door on the landing." He slung the cloth over his shoulder and pointed with the goblet.

Calling his thanks, Brick crossed the tavern floor and walked up the wooden staircase. *First door.* He opened it, thinking afterward he should have knocked, waited for an answer. But he didn't, just walked in...and stopped.

Because the most beautiful man he'd ever seen was lying on the bed. He was long and slim, with shapely arms and legs. He had an old-fashioned-looking mustache and small beard that probably had some fancy name Brick didn't have a clue about.

His dark eyes gleamed with intelligence and humor. His curly, dark shoulder-length hair fanned out onto his pillow and he was wearing sexy leather clothing, including a long duster coat and leather breeches.

It could have been any of those things that caught Brick's attention, but what he couldn't tear his gaze from and that had his mouth watering far, *far* more than the tavern's pie could ever, was that the man's breeches were undone, and he had his cock in his hand.

Chapter Six

"Don't be shy," Jagger called to whoever was at the door. He knew the picture he made, lying with his pants open, his billowing shirt framing his body as he gave lazy pulls on his dick. "Unless that's what does it for you." He wasn't that into roleplay, but if the man who'd sought him out wanted to indulge some 'wicked elf ravishing poor little me' fantasy, Jagger could get behind it. Or on top of it. *Whatever.* "I can't do much with you over there though, so..."

He trailed off when he got a look at the man who wanted an elf. The *huge* man, a stranger, his face kissed by the sun and his eyes shining gold. *Shifter,* Jagger could tell, in the kingdom for the celebrations, no doubt. What type of shifter was more difficult to say, with all the physic and remnants of spells clouding him, but Jagger wasn't about to demand a species certificate. He was here for a good fuck, the best way to forget the palace and all that came with it.

He'd fled the Great Hall as soon as he'd been able, without so much as a glimpse of his 'intended'. Oh, he'd tried to get one, but the wyverns' table had been hazed in some shielding magic—did the youngest, his groom-to-be, have zits they were ashamed of? And so here he was, his usual haunt, where he never had to wait long for a companion to fuck the hours away with. Someone like this, a stranger, probably curious to discover if what they said about elves was true.

Well, no, there'd never been anyone quite like *this*. This sexalicious tall and broad stranger, who got even more blood pumping to Jagger's cock, what with the way he filled out the…two sets of clothes he was wearing. "Cold?" Jagger inquired.

The guy shook his head. No, Jagger bet he was as hot as he looked.

"Got a name to go with that gorgeous bod?" Jagger slid from the bed, unable to take his eyes from the stranger.

"Bri— Sim. Sim," the man answered.

"Well, Sim, let's get you naked," Jagger said, stripping Sim as fast as he could. "Why so many clothes?"

"Because I'm stupid," Sim answered, his face turned down.

It intrigued Jagger. He bent a little to get his face under Sim's. "I don't think you're stupid," he whispered, his mouth against Sim's ear. He gave it a lick, seeing as he was there, pleased when Sim shivered where he stood. "I think you're sexy as fuck."

He wondered why Sim looked surprised at that. He must know how edible he was, with that strong, handsome face and the way he peeped up from under those thick bronzed-gold lashes that framed those seductive yellow-gold—*gods above and below*—slitted eyes!

Sim stood, never taking his gaze from Jagger's as he undressed him to discover all that solid, thick, tan muscle inch by inch and, when Jagger tore open his pants, a massive cock and full balls.

"Oh, I'm going to enjoy this," Jagger breathed. "Or more accurately, I'm going to enjoy *you*. And I guarantee this'll be the best fuck you've ever had. Take that off." He'd left Sim in an undershirt, and now leaned back to track the flex of Sim's muscles when he tugged off the garment. "What is *that*?" Fascinated, Jagger pointed at the golden ring through Sim's right nipple.

"Piercing."

"Through the *flesh*?" Jagger came close to see. "What…? *Why?*"

Sim flushed an even sexier duskier shade. "I was drunk. Out with my friends. It's—"

"Sensitive?" Jagger picked up the thought somehow, and his eyes widened at Sim's nod. "Can I—?"

"How about you undressing as well?" Sim interrupted. "And tell me your name?"

Name? He had one, he was sure, but Sim bending to pull down his pants then bending more to yank them off, showcasing a spectacular ass that would make a unicorn weep, sent his mind blank. Jagger took himself behind Sim to feast his eyes a little more on those taut, firm yet ample spheres.

Sim's build and physique told the tale of an active life, but Jagger couldn't see him farming or fishing. More like he was a guard or warden, charged with the safety of whatever delegation he was in the kingdom to accompany, but then again, Jagger wasn't exactly interviewing him for a job. He could think of a few positions he'd like Sim in, though. A few gaps he could fill…

Jagger shrugged out of his shirt, his body heating with arousal.

"Well?" Sim asked, spinning around to face front again.

Jagger had no objection—this view was mouth-watering too. Literally. He could almost taste that thick cock, feel it flattening his tongue already, and the mere thought had his blood rushing to his own boner, pumping it bigger than it had ever been before. "Oh, yeah," he muttered, taking his pants off, pleased when Sim's gaze burned him.

"What's your n—?"

"Murstyn." It came out automatically. He generally used the names of the older, more dried-up councilors with strangers, so they'd go back to their lands and spread tales of how well-fucked Hareth had left their ass, or how much Jomb had loved eating them out. He was doing the court a favor, he'd always reasoned. "Now can I?"

He didn't wait for answer but fondled the gold hoop piercing Sim's flat nipple, delighting in the hiss Sim gave at even this relatively innocent contact. Jagger turned the ring in a circle, feeling how the metal warmed as it passed through Sim's flesh. Doing this brought his finger and thumb to the nub itself and he rubbed a thumb over it. "Does it hurt?" he asked.

"Not enough," Sim replied, and his words, uttered in that deep voice, hit Jagger like a lash.

Manticores bite me… Jagger tugged at the hoop, pulling it away and stretching the nipple, first with his fingers then with his teeth. He used his tongue tip to almost flip the gold circle, pushing it flat against the skin above Sim's nip instead of letting it hang below. Keeping it there, like a frame, he poked his tongue through it to tickle Sim's nub. Sim threw out a hand, catching at the tall chest of drawers to steady himself, and it made his muscles bunch nicely.

So nicely, in fact, that Jagger thought he'd better check them out, should smooth his hands over Sim's thick chest with the perfect dusting of hair, and the sculpted planes of his shoulders. Maybe even draw his nails down his warm skin a little…

"That's what you like." Sim seemed pleased at his discovery. "Chests and arms."

"Oh, I like plenty of other parts too," Jagger assured him.

"Like this?" With his golden eyes, with their fascinating vertical slit pupils, still gazing into Jagger's, Sim fondled his erect dick.

"I wouldn't say no…" Jagger took over from Sim, stroking the thick, hard ridge of his cock, which was so full, he could hardly close his hand around it. Changing things up, he drew his thumb over the head, leaving it shiny with pre-cum that he slicked in a fat circle. Another bubble appeared at the tip as he watched. Jagger was just about to taste it when Sim spoke.

"Harder. I like it—"

"Rough?" Jagger could hardly believe his luck, after the shitty time he'd had of it today, that Sim, a strong, thick-muscled shifter, was into the hard, wild sex Jagger liked. Sim nodded. "Show me."

Licking his lips, Sim knocked Jagger's hand from his cock then circled its length himself, his strokes fast and hard. He reached for Jagger and palmed his erection too. Jagger took in a deep breath at the grip of Sim's fingers. The stretch of the tendons in his hand struck

Jagger as winglike, somehow. *Dragon,* he mused, and then, at the first stroke Sim gave to his dick, Jagger wasn't thinking anymore, just reacting. Need filled him, took him over, and he stepped away.

"You got a nice cock," Sim said.

He had to smile at Sim's praise. "Thanks. I like it." Sim's open appreciation made him harder. "You will too." He trailed his gaze down Sim's body to make his meaning clear. In case it wasn't, he added, "When it's buried in your ass, and I'm fucking the breath from your body."

"I want a kiss first."

"You w—?" Jagger started to ask, then it was Sim's turn to make himself clear—he grabbed Jagger to bring him closer. Jagger clutched back and their meeting became a clash of lips and teeth and a battle for dominance of tongues. It wasn't just one slicking over another but a devouring, a *taming,* one Jagger won only, he felt, because Sim let him. *Good.* His arousal grew.

Sim touched his fingers to his face. "Never kissed a man with a mustache and beard before."

"It'll feel even better on the insides of your thighs," Jagger promised, enjoying this back and forth. And he didn't even have his dick in the guy's ass yet. "And when I suck your balls, you'll probably come in my face."

Sim's answer to that was to widen his stance, spreading his legs as if Jagger would kneel between them and get to it. Oh, he would. Burning with arousal so hot that he wondered if his fingers were scorching Sim, he spun him around and gave a sharp nip to the back of his neck. He didn't know why he did it—it wasn't one of his usual moves, but it allowed him to scrape his beard across Sim's skin.

Jagger didn't have a long beard, like Hust's. His barely covered his chin and was fashioned into a neat point in an old-fashioned style that he'd made new again, like he had with his equally neat mustache. And Sim's long, noisy inhalation said he was enjoying the feel of both under his ear and trailing down to that delicious crease where neck met shoulder. Jagger scratched into Sim's hair too, enjoying the springy feel of the short fuzz that was softer than it looked.

He ran his nails down Sim's broad back. "God, I'm looking forward to being inside you," he admitted. He was never this desperate, always had better control, but there was something about this tall, broad yet gentle and soft man that destroyed him. That could *wreck* him. Well, Jagger was along for the ride. Would even steer…

He pushed Sim two steps to the room's sturdy wooden table and bent him over it, then slid down his body, digging his nails deeper into Sim's warm, tan flesh as he went, to end on the floor, kneeling between his strong legs. He caressed them, running his hands up the flesh that pebbled in his wake to cup Sim's plush ass cheeks, loving how they flexed in his palms. He darted his tongue up the cleft between them, a quick, exploratory touch, and Sim started.

"What?" Jagged asked. "I have to get you prepped. You got a better way in mind?"

"No," Sim replied after a pause, and jiggled his ass in Jagger's face.

"Didn't think so." Jagger gave Sim's ass a slap to prove his point.

Chapter Seven

Gods, his butt was so firm it didn't jiggle even one bit on being slapped. The guy was built—he could take a hard reaming. Maybe next time— Jagger caught up with what he was thinking and frowned. *Already planning another session?* That wasn't like him, and the guy was a one-and-done, an elf-fucker who'd come to get his fill…which Jagger would make sure he did.

He kneaded the firm flesh that filled his palms. His erection was raging by now, demanding he did something about it, but he ignored it, wanting to do this for Sim instead. He parted the ass cheeks he was clasping, exposing Sim's pucker. "Gods' truth, you have the sweetest ass," Jagger commented, nuzzling from the top of Sim's crease down to his hole.

"How would you know?" Sim gave an impatient wriggle.

"Good point." He hadn't tasted it yet. "And talking of points, here comes another…" Jagger firmed the tip of his tongue and used both hands to spread Sim's cheeks farther, to lap then lave at his pucker. "Yeah, sweet," he muttered indistinctly, his face buried and his tongue and lips busy. "Guess you're from somewhere where rimming's a thing, right?"

He wondered where Sim was from…and what his real name was. 'Sim' wasn't talking at the moment, though, just gripping hard to the sides of the table, his knuckles whiter than the rest of his hands. It fired Jagger up to continue and he did, with gusto, putting plenty of slurp and saliva in it, making it as filthy as possible. He loved eating a guy out and could do it for as long as a partner could stand it.

Sim's upper body was flat to the table and he was pressing down, trying to get traction on his cock, and pushing back, trying to fuck himself on Jagger's tongue. He'd already reached the needing something deeper in his ass stage. Gods, he was responsive.

Jagger pulled Sim's hips away from the table's edge, though. Sim wasn't going to rub one out like that, no matter how desperate Jagger got him. *Soon.* He eased the tip of his tongue inside Sim's hole, to flicker it about the tight heat and test the resilience of the inner walls…and make Sim groan. *Good.* The sound did more than please Jagger—it set his soul alight.

Jagger pulled free to work the rim again, to make it soften for him. Pulling Sim's head up, he reached a hand around to his mouth, the fingers extended. "Wet them," he demanded through puffy lips.

Sim did, sucking and tonguing his fingers, even giving a tiny nip with his teeth before resting his head flat again. Jagger brought his hand back, to press the now slick fingers to Sim's hole. If his tongue had gotten it soft and pliant, his caressing, teasing the barest pressure inside, had it *pouting* for him, eager and willing. "Beautiful," Jagger murmured. Sim's ass was almost begging for him now and Sim was pushing back, blindly seeking more penetration.

"Need lube." Jagger had dreams about fucking a guy from a species where self-lubricating asses were real and not just a fantasy that young elves drooled over, but he hadn't met one so far. He couldn't tear himself away though, not without running his nails up that broad back laid out for him, making the muscles quiver and the flesh blush.

He was back from the chest of drawers within seconds, slicking his cock with one lube-smeared hand and Sim's hole with the other. *And they say at council meetings I'm incapable of focusing on more than one thing at a time.* "Okay?" he asked, but anything else he wanted to ask or say vanished into the ether at the sight of Sim's face, turned to one side on the table and those golden eyes fixed on him.

"I'll be better when you fuck me," the shifter spread out for Jagger's pleasure said.

"Wait…" Jagger darted to close the viewing panels on the far wall and slid the bolts home. He'd never minded anyone watching him perform, but this…wasn't a performance. *Just mine. Just for me and no one else.* Unable to wait another second, he lined his cock up with Sim's hole and pressed in, almost jumping at the loud cry this wrenched from Sim.

"*Godssss,*" Jagger hissed at the sight of his girth spearing and opening Sim up, at the tight resistance he had to breach and the heat and constriction that met him when he did so. Being inside Sim, and Sim's vocal and physical response to Jagger's cock in his ass, drove him wild. He leaned over to scratch the length of Sim's back again and this time had the sensation of scales and ridges under his fingers, but when he looked, only smooth bronzed flesh met his gaze.

As he bottomed out, he leaned low to again bite the back of Sim's neck and this made his partner arch…which meant two things. One, that his ass pushed back harder into Jagger, and two, that Jagger could get a hand under his torso and play with his nipple ring. A moan left Sim when Jagger gave a tug on the golden ring in time with his thrust into Sim's tight channel.

Curving over, needing to see Sim's face, Jagger gasped at the sight of his eyes. Still fixed on his, the pupils were thin lines of black in the dark yellow, and Jagger had an image of dark wings beating against a sky of gold. It was more than an image—it was the sensation of flight, effortless and high in the air.

As that picture entered his mind, Sim's ass clamped tighter and harder than before around Jagger's dick, forcing a long moan from the bottom of Jagger's lungs. He pulled his cock out to the head, then slammed back in. The high-pitched sound Sim made was nearer to a shriek than anything else, and he wriggled, then struggled, trying to get his hand to his cock.

"No." Jagger was there before him, angling his hips back to get his own hand in place and ring the base of Sim's massive erection, the tight band of his fingers preventing Sim from coming. He withdrew from the clutch of Sim's ass, ignoring his cry of protest, then rammed back in, *hard,* his balls slapping against Sim's flesh.

Jagger wanted to play longer, but the clench of Sim's sheath on his cock and the way Sim moved onto him, meeting each thrust, echoing Jagger's panted cries, stoked his release. He only managed to drive into Sim twice more, unable to keep his hold on the shifter's sweat-dewed hip, when his release broke over him and he tumbled headfirst into it. His cum burst from him, flooding Sim's ass.

"Gods above," he panted.

"And below," his partner in pure, perfect sin replied. His frustrated partner, taking advantage of Jagger's trip into white-hot ecstasy to rut against the table.

"No..." Jagger pulled out, his cum dripping from Sim as he did so. Well, he'd shot a heavy load into him. He managed to keep his hold on Sim's dick until he'd backed him to the bed, where he shoved him onto it.

Sim's fall, broken by his elbows, slid his cock free of Jagger's hand. No sooner had Sim landed than Jagger pounced, straddling him to replace his hand with his mouth. He was curious. Dragons had ridges circling the length of their cocks, but Sim's dick had felt as smooth as a fairy's. He licked Sim from root to head and sucked at the leaking slit. His eyes rolled back in his head at the taste of the pre-cum. Sweet as nectar and as heady as wine, it left a spicy aftertaste on his tongue and made his head swim. It also had his cock filling again.

He didn't understand the word Sim shouted but understood the grip of Sim's hands in his hair, the way his fingers speared to the roots. He took Sim as deep as he could, his sheer size filling Jagger's mouth as satisfactorily as he'd envisioned...and more.

His dick didn't seem as smooth as it had. It wasn't ridged, as Llan's or Rhett's had been, when he'd enjoyed being the ringmaster and star in a dragon-sex circus. This had...bands? He grinned. "I never knew about this feature, but I want to know more. Know it from the inside. As in, I *really* hope you like to top, because I need these bumps in my rump."

"Oh, I do," Sim got out. "Not bumps—"

Whatever they were, Jagger tonguing them had Sim squirming on the mattress, and the head of his gloriously banded cock thickening even more in Jagger's mouth.

"Murstyn..."

It took Jagger a second to realize Sim was crying out his fake name.

"Let me come..."

Jagger nodded, which bobbed his head down more. He sucked harder, and Sim jetted down his throat with a roar louder than any shifter Jagger had ever heard. The stream was hot and even more ambrosial that the pre-cum, and for once Jagger couldn't swallow everything his talented tongue had called forth. He eased off and stroked Sim through the last pulses and damn if the sight of Sim, his tan body dripping in sweat and flushed an imperial red as he writhed and cried out and fought to keep his sunburst eyes open didn't have Jagger wanting to go again.

Then Sim's eyes opened wide, and Jagger gasped—he was flying. Well, not really—the cotton sheets were still under his knees and shins—but he felt the beat of wide wings under him, saw the ground falling away. He stared back. "What...?" he started but stopped.

Magic. Or something. Something that had him tingling all over, all through. Brick dropped his gaze and swung his leg over, to leave the bed, but he was prevented. The elf's weight on him knocked him flat onto his stomach, and the arm and leg quickly hooked over him kept him in place.

"We're not done yet," Murstyn said, into Brick's ear. He should leave, but it was hard to do that when Murstyn was already fucking him again, softly, effortlessly, using his cum for lube and sending pleasure coursing through him in nonstop streams. The occasional sharper jolt had Brick twitching as though lightning were striking him, and he chased each bolt like an addict scrabbling for poppy flowers.

And it was hard to leave after that too, when he was slipping in and out of sleep, his elf still a part of him.

Chapter Eight

Brick woke with the elf's cock still in him. Or in him *again*—he wasn't sure. What he did know was that it was the best wake-up he'd ever had. Glossy dark curls tickled his throat and upper chest from where his elf was taking slow, occasional nips at his neck. That little beard and mustache stimulated him so nicely—Murstyn had been dead-on about how it would feel on his balls. He lay as still as he could, his body supported in its half-on-its-side and half-on-its-stomach collapse by a strong arm around his waist, the fingers snaking up to his upper chest.

Murstyn—or whatever his real name is—is sure fascinated by my pierced nipple. The attention he'd paid to it made Brick regret he hadn't gotten that cock piercing he'd been thinking about. Flad had, and boasted of it often, and his hook-ups were very appreciative of it.

Behind him, his elf stretched the gold hoop away from Brick's nip and huffed out a soft laugh, probably at the way this simple action made Brick's breath leave his body on a squeaky sigh. After a few minutes, the hand left its playground and trailed lower, to Brick's rising-and-shining cock, working it in time with the almost lazy rolls of the elf's hips.

About to say he'd never woken up like this before, Brick stilled. Why did the cock in his ass—an elf's cock—feel *banded,* like a *wyvern's*? He went to pull away when he noticed the hand working his cock looked different from the strong, long-fingered elf hand that had brought him so much pleasure all night.

His heart jolted at his thought that Murstyn had invited a third into their bed to fuck him and was trading off with a shifter. Was maybe sitting across the room, watching, about to join in. Or maybe someone had decided to take the elf's place—Murstyn had gone for breakfast and someone had slipped in and...*slipped in.* Was screwing Brick without either him or the elf knowing?

No. Even without turning round he knew who was behind him in the bed. He looked down at the hand again, and his blood chilled. It was the elf's...but with what looked like a wyvern's superimposed on it, like a phantom image. Then, as if a mist had cleared, Murstyn's hand was back and his dick, buried deep in Brick's channel, stopped feeling banded. *What is this?*

He must have been unnaturally still because the elf stopped moving too. "What's wrong?" he asked.

"I..." No, Brick had no clue how to explain. "I ran away from the palace because I'm being given to some geriatric, dried-up council member as part of a treaty," was what fell from his mouth. "I'm a wyvern—"

The elf pulled out so quickly there was a *pop.* He leaped from the bed, and Brick spun around to face him.

"The youngest son of the ruling family," he finished for Brick, his brown eyes flashing and his hair a glorious tangle of mahogany waves around his shoulders. It was messy enough to allow the just slightly pointed tips of his ears to peep through, like they were doing it on purpose to entice Brick. They had last night, and Brick had answered their call, discovering in his fondling that elf's ears were erogenous zones. Gods, he was fucking sexy and fun and clever and…

No. Please. No. Brick raised a shaking hand. "You're not—?"

"The geriatric councilor being forced into marriage with you?" the elf spat. "Yep, that'd be me."

"*Ogre shit!*" Brick yelped at the same time as his promised-one cried, "*Troll piss!*"

"Was this some fucking strategy?" the elf demanded. "Your wily wyvern family planned this out?"

"Funny—I was just gonna ask you if it was some palace power move. Some game playing." Brick swung his legs to the floor and stood.

The elf stared narrow-eyed at him. "Your zits cleared up well."

"What?" Brick could have done without this frosting of confusion spread on top of the base layer of misunderstanding. "I haven't had zits for several years. Not since that treatment Scarlet sent off for, the one with the virgin pixie semen harvested at new moon." He sighed. "I really did run away when I learned yesterday what the plan was. The alliance thing. The treaty-seal. The whole me being handed over—"

"To some dried-up old man. Yes, got that. And nothing dry about me."

True—his cock gleamed wet from his cum from their last go-around or his pre-cum in anticipation of his next climax. Brick wasn't sure which and didn't really want to ask. "I'm Brick, youngest son of the Ruby Throne." He held out his hand.

"Jagger. Royal-adjacent elf."

It felt odd to be shaking hands after they'd touched and fucked other body parts, and Jagger's smile said he thought so too. He had beautiful lips, framed so sexily by that long slim mustache and well-groomed triangle of beard. He was very good-looking and quick-witted, sexually adventurous and free and near the top of things elf-kingdom wise…making the very thought of him being tied to Brick cruel.

"Don't take this the wrong way, but this alliance—" they both said together and stopped.

"It's wrong," Brick finished. "Obviously. You, and me?" He scoffed.

"Yes. I can't," Jagger agreed. "I mean, I do feel a strong pull to you, even though I've had you, but settling down, all dull and dutiful, wasn't in my plans, you know? I'm a free spirit and… Wait. You said *wrong*?"

Of course he doesn't want to be with me. "I did." Brick looked for his clothes.

"It must be!" Jagger grabbed Brick's arm. "The prophecy, that says we're the ones who have to make this match, this deal—"

"You can't badmouth a prophecy!" Brick took a quick look around to see if any gods or spirits or *anything* were listening.

"Not the prophecy itself, but the interpretation. It's being read wrong. Misunderstood."

Oh. Brick considered that as he found his pants—both pairs—and pulled them on. "So if it is, you don't have to..." *Throw your life away on a big useless oaf like me.* "What does it say? Do you know? Did they read it out?"

"I didn't exactly take much in, what with being in shock," Jagger replied over his shoulder, hunching over to yank on his leather breeches.

Brick had to force himself to stop ogling. *But those tumbling curls. That slim body. That ass.* At least he'd have some knee-trembling memories to carry with him on his journey.

"So you ran away too? You didn't get far," he commented.

"*I* didn't run away. I know my sworn duty to my liege. I just had to get out. I needed to clear my head."

"Yeah, but which head?" Snorting, Brick indicated the messy tavern room, the soiled bed, the plate empty of the apfels and koza cheese they'd pigged out on to replenish their energy and the flagon of redberry-wine they'd drained when their fun had left them thirsty.

"Fine, so I needed a good fuck. Which you were, by the way. But *you're* judging *me*, flyboy? Seriously?" Jagger folded his arms across his chest.

That this stupidly sexy elf thought him a good fuck warmed Brick through. "No. Yes. A bit. I don't know! Look, we need to know what the foretelling says." Brick found his boots and jammed one on. It was the wrong one for that foot, so, blushing, he yanked it off again.

"They gave me a copy." Jagger brandished a rolled-up scroll tied with jade ribbon, and he and Brick pulled stools out from underneath the table, the same table where Jagger had...and then later had... His face hot now, Brick bent over the parchment that Jagger was smoothing flat.

"'In the time of dread, ancient Jade shall join with young Ruby red. In the time of fight, to strengthen both, Red and Jade must unite. Both are born to aid the Throne and the Storm,'" Brick read, his voice rising in incredulity as he got to the end. "It doesn't even *rhyme*! Or scan!"

"They never fucking do!" Jagger raged. "I'm always saying that! But that…it's as vague as a horoscope in an elfling picture-parchment. You know, like, 'be bold and decisive today and see what new direction opens up for you next week'."

Brick agreed, grinning at the high-pitched teenage voice Jagger put on. "Well, talking of bright, the words 'Ruby' and 'Throne' must mean the Ruby Throne, right?"

"You're a scholar, I see." Jagger ran his finger along another line. "I wonder what all these references to jade could mean, then?"

"The elf kingdom. Jade's the royal color, right? Oh. You were taking the piss." Brick looked down.

"Hey."

He met Jagger's gaze.

"Sorry. That was wrong of me." Jagger blew out a sigh. "I get sarcastic when I'm irritated but if I'm being a jerk, tell me."

Gods' ears and whiskers. Brick had to put his hand over his mouth to hide the smile that pulled up his lips. "So…you're ancient then?" He tapped the word in the foretelling.

"Not so old I can't kick your ass."

"You did that. Oh wait, you said 'kick'?" Brick couldn't resist it. He sniggered, delighted when Jagger joined in too. A sudden noise came from the floor below. "What's that?" Brick turned toward the door as if that would enable him to see what was causing the racket downstairs.

"Where is he?" an enraged male voice shouted, his fury cracking through the air.

Brick couldn't catch full sentences after that, but "that arrogant bastard sticking his cock where it doesn't belong" had him turning to Jagger. "It's for you."

"*Jagger!*" A female voice came from the panel in the wall, near the floor, and Jagger threw it open.

"What, Bette?" he asked.

A woman stuck her face out of the large hole. Brick thought he remembered seeing her behind the bar. "How comes you got Almighty Mallon all riled up? He's got a posse of his dock workers with him!"

The commotion grew louder, and Brick swallowed the questions trembling on his lips.

"Better run for it," Bette advised.

"Oh, he might be the most powerful trader and merchant in town, but Hust won't let him up here." Jagger tossed an apfel into the air, caught it, then took a bite.

"True…unless Mallon's threatening the Cock's spirits supply if Hust don't hand you over…and turn a blind eye to what he does." Bette vanished.

Footsteps thudded on the staircase.

"Dung! Better leg it." Jagger buckled on his sword belt and bent low to the escape tunnel Bette had used, then appeared to think better of it and straightened again.

"What? What's happening?" Brick looked from the tunnel to the door and back to Jagger who, snatchel slung across him, had one leg thrown over the windowsill.

"What's it look like? We're fleeing," Jagger replied.

"*We?*" Brick gaped.

"Yes. Unless you want to face *that*." Jagged pointed toward the tumult with a dagger as he said the last word, then shoved the blade into an ankle sheath. "If not, come on!"

He vanished and, cursing, Brick grabbed as many of his spare clothes as he could then took a running jump and followed.

Chapter Nine

"*Owww!*" he cried when he landed.

Jagger had no doubt Brick would have managed more, if Jagger, lying on his back underneath him, hadn't wrapped his hand around his mouth to shut him up.

"Anyone should be yelling in pain, it's me!" he hissed in Brick's ear. "With me having broken your fall, you bog wanderer! Why in the seven hells did you jump out of the fucking window when we're two floors up? Why didn't you climb down that pipe right there like I did?"

He regretted his words when Brick hung his head and muttered something against Jagger's muffling hand. All Jagger could catch of it was the word *stupid*. Brick had called himself that last night, and Jagger didn't like it. He didn't agree with it, either. Brick was witty and sharp. It wasn't his fault he didn't know the tavern's…amenities.

"Guess it proves you haven't had as much practice as me at fleeing from things like this," he said.

"I bet no one has," Brick twisted round to reply. "You must be a gold medalist at it."

His sly humor had Jagger almost forgiving him his crash landing and his elbows digging into Jagger's stomach. "We'd better move," he said, shifting his hips to illustrate why—Brick in his lap was getting him hard.

Brick leaped to his feet, and Jagger shoulder-shoved him into the shelter of the wall where they'd be less visible for Brick to finish dressing. "Sorry," Brick muttered.

"Never apologize for straddling my crotch." Jagger grinned. "Come on." He led the way around the side of the tavern to the alley at the back.

"What did you do?" Brick asked, following to the end of the alley. "If a posse's gonna set on me, I should know why."

As if his words had called them, two large broad men, hired mercenaries by the look of them, hurried from the tavern's back door and chased down the narrow passage after them.

"Jagger—"

"Not a problem," he assured Brick, hoping it wasn't. They were beside the small storeroom used for warehousing the tavern's stocks, and he turned into it, Brick so close behind him that his breath heated Jagger's neck. If he turned his head just slightly, that breath would mist across his ear tip and— *Gods! This isn't the time!*

Wrenching his mind from thoughts of sex, Jagger raced through the building and out of the back exit. It gave onto the market square, which bustled with people, vendors and buyers, and rang with their cries and chatter. Jagger pulled Brick behind the end stall of a short row that sold clothes.

The long dresses displayed on high poles and fluttering in the morning breeze provided some cover, and the young woman whose business it was winked and looked away, busying herself laying out woolen stockings.

"Don't look!" Jagger yanked Brick back from where he was peering out. He sighed at the questioning look Brick still wore. He obviously wanted to know why some guy was chasing Jagger. Well, Jagger and Brick, now. "It was a difference of opinion about…a seduction," he half-explained.

"*Hey!*" yelled a man's voice a second before there came a crash—a pera fruit farmer's stall had been shoved aside, his green and yellow fruit tumbling everywhere. Jagger whipped around, guessing what he would find.

"Seize that vile defiler of decent people's innocent sons!"

Mallon the Merchant was flanked by the huge men from the alley, making him look shorter and squatter than ever, just as his anger and the exertion made his face more toadlike. He glared and shook the cane he carried at any townsfolk who dared to call out a criticism or jeer him.

"I wouldn't have thought he'd be your type." Brick, his lip curled, looked from Mallon to Jagger. "No, don't tell me—you lost a bet?"

"That's not him! That's his *father*, you bridge troll." But Jagger grinned.

"Face me like an elf should!" Mallon demanded.

"I am—like any sensible elf should," Jagger retorted, sprinting through the stalls for open ground, grabbing

Brick's sleeve to make sure he kept up. He didn't need to be concerned—Brick was fit and had great stamina, as Jagger knew from last night and this morning. A glance behind him showed him Mallon directing his goons like a man used to getting other people to do his dirty work. Jagger sped up.

They darted into a store and out through the side exit into a street, their paces well matched. Jagger slowed, taking stock of where they were. They were coming up to a grassy strip, a small leisure area with a few ornamental flower beds, but as soon as they set foot on it, Jagger felt uneasy.

"Think we got away!" Brick exclaimed. "If he's still after us, he must be all the way back there and can't touch us."

"But maybe he has something else that can..." Jagger pointed to a row of small brown lumps in the ground just ahead of them. They could have been mushrooms, growing very quickly from the earth, but they weren't. The knobbly things were— "Hobgoblins. Thugs for hire," he added, in case they didn't have them in the wyvern lands.

"Those tiny gnomes?" Brick snickered. "They look as small as pixies."

"Pixies don't carry gnarled clubs about the same size as their bodies," Jagger observed as the row of creatures finished tugging themselves from the earth and advanced on them, clubs and all.

"Want me to stomp on them for you so you don't ruin your swashbuckler boots?" Brick was still laughing, but the grin slid off his face when the thugs charged, not clubbing them, but pulling burrs from their pockets and throwing them at him and Jagger in a fusillade.

"Dragons' dangles!" yelped Brick, slapping at his leg where a burr had hit him. He rubbed at another, then a third, backing away. "That *burns*."

"Only burns?" Jagger's teeth were still chattering from the shock that had zinged through him when a series of red burrs had made contact with him, one after the other. Another hit had his hair sizzling. The flank of hobgoblins to the right plucked brown burrs from their stupid round caps...and these pierced, sticking where they hit, he discovered.

The noise attracted an audience, a whole clump of townspeople hurrying up to witness the spectacle, laughing and pointing and calling out advice. Elves loved a hobbling, unless they were the victims, of course.

"Stop!" Brick begged the smirking creatures, who were now warming up their clubs by swinging them around with a horrible whistling sound and slapping them into the palms of their free hands. They ignored him—if anything his plea goaded them into marching forward, a shouting, clobbering melee.

"This is humiliating," Jagger said through clenched teeth. Word was bound to spread of it, for sure. The shame was part of it. He just hoped none of his fellow councilors could see him at this moment.

"If any of my teammates find out about this, they'll laugh me off the tail ball squad," Brick said, echoing his thoughts.

"Back to back," Jagger and Brick told each other at the same time, looking at the other in surprise, then sliding round so they each faced outward.

"We have got to stop doing that," Jagger commented on their tendency to say the same thing, to be thinking the same thing, then spared his breath for stomping and punching—necessary when the back line of hobs jumped onto the first row's shoulders, increasing their height.

And decreasing their stability—they were easier to knock off and flatten as they wobbled. Stamping on them both shrank and compressed the hobgoblins, although it was very unpleasant to squash them underfoot and the squishing and shattering sounds were awful. Jagger was glad when each crushed body seeped back into the earth. The only good thing about it was Brick's solid warmth against his, with the feeling of support he provided.

"I think that's it!" panted Brick, sounding as exhausted as Jagger felt. "Oh..."

Jagger, heart sinking at that syllable, whirled around to see three more lines of toadstool-like caps emerging from the ground. "Mallon must have paid for the deluxe service," he commented.

"Hope his son was worth it," Brick said, an odd note in his voice.

"Not really," Jagger had to confess. The hobgoblins' lumpy brown faces were free of the earth now.

"They look like potatoes." Brick took a step back. "And I like potatoes. *Liked*. You're ruining potatoes for me!" he yelled at the hobs, scowling when the audience laughed.

Wait. Earth. The earth was one space, and the sky another. "What say we make a quick and stylish getaway, leave all this behind?" Jagger muttered to Brick. "Or, I should say, leave it all below?"

Brick frowned at him, and Jagger rolled his eyes. "Can't you fly?" he asked, flapping his arms and pointing upward.

"I..." Too many emotions flickered across Brick's face for Jagger to catch, but the final one, *speculation*, he got. Brick sniffed, then stuck his tongue out and rubbed his forehead and pinched his nose.

"Please tell me this is your pre-flight warm up," Jagger begged, pointing to where the ranks of hobs stamped their feet, chittering and admiring one another's clubs that had nails sticking out of them. *Talk about deluxe.* "Please— *Fuck!*"

The last word came out in a yelp, because where Brick had stood was a huge, winged beast. A wyvern, resplendent in sun-kissed hues that took Jagger's breath away. He stood gawking, until the wyvern—Brick—nudged him off-balance, making Jagger clutch at his sinuous neck, which was when Brick dipped, to get Jagger on his back.

A second later they were airborne, accompanied by a loud trumpeting, blasting noise and a cloud of noxious gas. Jagger grabbed for something to hold on to as he scrambled to a sitting position from the undignified face-down sprawl he'd landed across Brick in and looked below.

"You didn't—You *did*! You just farted on those hobgoblins!" he exclaimed, watching them fall to the ground like ninepins hit by a wrecking ball. "I knew your ass was damn fine, but enough to bowl that many creatures over in one go? You..."

Are gorgeous. Jagger stroked a ridge on the spine of the long, lithe body whose tawny, dusky shades evoked thoughts of exotic far-off lands with hot sands and burning suns. The thick tendons of Brick's powerful wings stretched and relaxed, propelling them through the air, and within seconds, Jagger's heart beat in time with the rise and fall. *I've dreamed this,* he thought.

No, it couldn't have been a dream—he'd been awake. *I've* felt *this,* he self-corrected. But...how was that possible?

Chapter Ten

Jagger didn't understand, but loved the sensation, the feeling of freedom that he hadn't known he was lacking, that he hadn't realized his soul had been craving. The wide-open space, the rush of the air, the strength and power between his thighs. *Well, a little more power between my thighs than usual.* He laughed as his hair streamed behind him in the breeze. He had no idea where they were going and didn't think Brick did either—he was taking them in wide circles over the same terrain.

"You heading anywhere in particular?" he asked, to check, and had to clutch hard to stay seated when Brick's body undulated in what could only be a shrug.

"Warn me next time you do that!" Jagger demanded, righting his snatchel and sword. "And you'd better not be planning on looping the loop, or I'll have your hide to make new boots from."

But he couldn't be irritated, not up high like this, with the rumble of Brick's laughter rippling under him, making his balls tingle. *Gods, imagine riding him naked,* he thought, already feeling the tickle of the feathers and the press of the ridges on his inner thighs and taint. As he envisioned that, Brick turned his broad head slowly on his long neck, to level a look at Jagger from his golden eyes.

"Wait. Wyverns can't…can they? You're not reading my mind, right?" Jagger gasped.

Brick blinked a few times, the hoods above his eyes sweeping down. He seemed agitated, jerking his head.

"Look, I'll keep my clothes on," Jagger promised.

Brick thrust his head out to turn them in a tight semi-circle, so they were facing the direction they'd come in…giving Jagger a clear view of the pair of dark birds coming up fast on them.

"Okay. Got it now. And that part about me riding you naked…" He trailed off when the two large shiny birds caught them up and launched straight into the attack, lashing out with their metallic beaks. Letting out an indignant hiss, Brick swerved, to avoid having his flesh ripped off, and Jagger grabbed wildly, to avoid being thrown off.

"*Stymph birds?*" Jagger's incredulity was because the fabled man-eating birds of prey, said to live beyond the lava pits in Planzatillo, on the other side of the world, were creatures of myth. *Fables.* Something fed-up big brothers and sisters used to keep a younger and fussy elfling in line, along the lines of, "*If you don't eat up all that cere gruel, stymph birds will peck you with their bronze beaks, fire their sharp metal feathers at you and crap on you with their poisonous dung.*"

Closer than he wanted to be to them, Jagger was able to verify that, yes, they had bronze beaks they used for pecking their prey. And yes again—he threw himself as flat as he could on Brick's back just in time—as they pinged off their own feathers, which twisted themselves around in midair and fired them at their victims.

That their feathers were made of metal wasn't an exaggeration either. One gave a sharp *ting* as its barb hit the dagger strapped to his ankle. Oh yes—he had a dagger and a sword and not inconsiderable prowess with both! He thrust his last weapons evaluation, the one that had claimed he had *more swagger than skill* out of his mind.

He stood, then decided against it when he fell immediately, landing on his balls. He'd trained on horseback, riding bareback, so he could grip with his knees and feint, lunge and parry with the best of them *and* with shiny metal birds. They were bigger than he'd imagined— Ah, because they swelled and grew as they engaged with an enemy, as though feeding on something.

As long as they don't feed enough to make dung. Because I really don't want to learn if that's a feature, too.

His ears rang from the sound of metal on metal when he struck a bird's beak with his sword. The recoil up his arm had him flat on his back, but he was too well trained to lose his grasp on his sword or his grip on his steed. And to think he'd bitched and moaned at getting up at first light to practice. If he had to do it all over again, he'd...still rather stay in bed. *And badmouth the shield mistress. Not to her face, obviously.* Everyone in the kingdom feared the Lady Lizabetta, and her sisters, Lady Lucinda and Lady Luella.

But the bird he'd fought had dropped back and was cawing indignantly and shaking his head, its feathers flicking off and floating harmlessly about it. "Take that!" Jagger called at it. "Try that again, and I'll pluck your plumage myself and stick you in a casserole."

Brick gave a wriggle, and Jagger knew it was a warning of some kind. He nodded, although Brick couldn't see him, not questioning how he understood Brick's meaning, or how Brick knew he'd understand too. He gripped a neck ridge, so that when Brick twisted his body almost in half to flail out his huge, long barbed tail, Jagger remained in place.

Not so the stymph—Brick scored a direct hit and the bird screeched, spinning in place from the force of the blow. Another direct hit would shatter it, rend its wings from its body, its beak from its head. But when Jagger, sword poised, braced himself for Brick to strike again, Brick instead turned to face the wounded creature.

Slow flaps of his wings kept Brick almost stationary in the air as he and the bird stared at each other, and the bird nodded and dropped back, leaving Brick and Jagger, a wyvern and an elf, in sole possession of the sky.

Until Brick fell. He plummeted, and Jagger was barely able to sheathe his sword and dagger with the speed of their descent. Brick flickered and shimmered, his body not as solid as it had been, then he shifted. From one heartbeat to the next, his wyvern form vanished and back once again was the tall, broad man Jagger had known him as first.

A falling version, with windmilling arms and scrabbling legs, as was Jagger, until they landed with two loud synchronised splashes, in a river below.

It wasn't deep or fast, and they both bobbed up immediately. Jagger's first thought was that the stymphs, as ineffectual as their attack had been for such feared creatures, had hurt Brick, to ruin his shift like that. The bigger the shifter, the more power they had, so Brick must have sustained a lot of damage, to have lost form and fallen from his element? Jagger grabbed Brick's arm, holding him still to look him over. He seemed okay but wouldn't meet Jagger's eyes.

"Why? Why didn't you kill that scabby-feathered piece of shit?" he demanded, spitting out water and flicking his wet hair from his eyes. "I'd have roasted it over a fire!"

"I don't like violence." Brick pulled some weed from his mouth, his hand a little shaky. "Although I feel like hitting you though, for bringing all this crap down on us."

"*What?*" Horrified, Jagger looked up, prepared to dive beneath the surface of the water. "Oh, Metaphorical crap. Look, I had no idea this was going to happen. It's not my fault." When Brick remained silent, waiting, Jagger sighed. "I'm sorry. I hope you're not hurt. And, as I recall saying to you before, that was some ride you gave me."

He took Brick's arm, helping him wade to the bank. "That was amazing. I've never done that before. And your shifted form was…something else."

"Yeah. A wyvern. You probably didn't recognize it, with the color—"

"Colors. So many…" Jagger was again lost in wonder at the beauty. Brick's color had changed as it went along his body, the hues shading so subtly into one another they rippled. He hoped he'd get the chance to study it properly. Or…improperly, with the thoughts he was having. "I've never seen anything so gorgeous," he told Brick. He levered himself out of the water and sat.

"Really? Huh. I'd say you should get out more, in that case, but…I know you get around." Brick followed suit.

"Variety is the spice of sex." Jagger squeezed water from his hair and looked about them. The field was deserted.

"That Mallon guy seemed like he had pepper up his ass," Brick agreed. "He must have some cash to hire muscle like that."

"He's rich, yeah. And pissed. He wanted his son to remain pure—virginity increases his worth in the marriage market." All the greedy merchant knew was commodities, buying and selling. "His son had other ideas."

"I see. But he wasn't worth it?" Brick wrung out his jacket.

Jagger gave a half-laugh. "Not really. I know some guys get off on being the first into an untapped ass, that breaking in a virgin is the thing that rings their bell, but busting cherries isn't really my thing."

"So why did you?"

"He asked," Jagger replied after a pause.

"I see. Well, this is not what I imagined when I decided to be a roving ambassador for my kingdom," Brick said after a pause, raising his dripping arms. "It's been…interesting, and you're welcome. For the ride, the rescue…"

About to argue, Jagger instead muttered, "Thanks." He pulled a pera fruit from his snatchel and offered it to Brick.

Brick took it and ate it in three bites, including the core. Shifting took a lot of energy. Jagger knew that from a cute little fox shifter he'd…met. One who liked to keep his fox tail, even in other-form. Even during sex.

Especially during sex. Oh, and his ears. Those cute little furry ears… Jagger held in a whine and willed his erection down. Were shifters what did it for him? No, the shifter next to him was doing it for him, even clothed and dripping wet.

Brick wiped his hands on the grass. "I guess we'd better get back to the palace, face the music."

Jagger hated the sad, resigned look Brick was wearing, and hated even more that Brick's life was going to be shitty because of him. *And vice versa,* he told himself. He was Jagger, the elf with the swagger, the kingdom's freest spirit who had no intention of being trapped into domesticity.

"What if we were to change the tune?" he asked. "Refuse to have our lives dictated by a stupid bit of doggerel no one's sure of the meaning of?"

"Yeah. I imagine that the thought of being tied to…" Brick busied himself tilting his head to tip water from his ear. "How?"

Jagger hadn't thought that far ahead. "Well, we could seek out the actual meaning of the prophecy?" he suggested.

"Oooh! Like by making our way to the Cave of the Worlds, where the fabric of the veil is thinner, and asking the Horrorcle there?" Brick stared at him.

"What? Talk about from a walk to a gallop! You're joking—?" He broke off, narrowing his eyes at the faint clucking noise he was sure he could hear. *Chicken?* Not Jagger. He should do this. If he could find out something to stop his life having its balls cut off, he would.

"We can fly right there, right?" And be back by the wedding—he didn't want to think of the consequences for missing it.

"Fly? Well…" Brick looked away.

Oh damn. Maybe losing flight was like losing an erection. Jagger didn't know much about shifters, but he knew a lot about cocks. "The cave's that way, isn't it?" He pointed east, toward the forest that was outside the elven realm, and Brick's mumbled, "Probably," didn't reassure him.

Jagger looked around for something to aid them, although what he was hoping to find, he didn't know. He thought quickly. He knew more or less where they were, basically just outside the capital. He also knew there was a small burg, a suburb of the capital, beyond this field, where there'd be people to help them.

"Are you thinking what I'm thinking?' he asked. "That river's flowing east. Elves have a saying, 'let the water do the work'…"

Brick looked from him to the river and back again, a huge grin lighting up his face. "Yeah," he agreed, and a second later had reached out and pushed Jagger in.

"*No!*" was all Jagger had time to yell before he hit the water. Again. And hitting it from a sitting position, head-first, with his mouth open meant he got a free drink of river slime. He surfaced and twisted around.

"Wh—?" he started to demand before he was splashed from head to torso by the wave Brick made by jumping in too. The river churned around them, picking up force, and swept them away from the bank.

"*Why?* Why did you do that?" Jagger raged, treading water.

"So we can get through the forest to the hills where the cave is, of course." Brick swirled past him, carried by a current. "Isn't that what you meant, we use the river to get there?"

"My idea, if you'd let me voice it, was to take ourselves to Brantle, a mile or so that way, and enjoy some rest and recreation, by which I mean more sex, while we pay someone to sail down the Welling River and do the job for us!" Jagger shook a fist at him, causing more splashes.

"Oh," Brick said. He looked at the fields on either side of the fast-running water then back at Jagger. "Oh. My bad."

Chapter Eleven

"Well, we're here now." Sloshing and dripping, Brick tried to make the best of it. He also tried to not ask Jagger if he thought, like Brick did, that the river sort of had them in its grip and was bearing them along. "What's this forest up ahead called?" he asked, hoping for something like the Playful Forest, or the Nice and Easy Forest or –

"The Forbidden Forest," came the watery reply.

Yeah, that was more along the lines of what he'd been expecting. "If it's forbidden, why's…? Nothing." *No.* He wouldn't voice his suspicions.

"Why is the water rushing us into it?" Jagger voiced them for him. "I don't know, but I'm guessing we'll find out."

"Haven't you ever been there?" Brick asked.

"I'm a courtier, a palace councilor, the son of the chancellor, grandson of the previous chancellor!" Jagger snapped.

"And?"

"And I'm a little bit too busy with my duties to the Storm King to go picnicking in forests!"

Brick wished he hadn't mentioned food. It made his stomach rumble, which made Jagger look up into the sky.

"Was that thunder? That's all we need."

At least it was only his stomach, and not…either end of his digestive tract this time. *Oh…* Nothing flatulence-related or nosebleed-related had happened when he'd shifted back there. Brick still didn't know how he'd been able to transform and take wing just now, not when magic danced in the air here, and faint sprinkles dusted this elf too.

Thank the gods it wasn't giving him a headache, just a feeling of heaviness in his brain. Well, maybe that was a result of the medicinal draft a servant had kindly fetched him from the palace healer yesterday. The tankard the page had presented to him had been full of a cool elixir…with smoke pouring from it, and Brick had guzzled it down in one.

It had left Brick not only feeling no pain whatsoever, but bold enough to decide to leave the Ruby Throne and make his own way in the world. For the first time, he wondered if he should have taken that entire draught with his other meds. *Oh well. A day late and a dwarf short.* And its effects would have worn off by now.

A strong sense of enchantment, as sharp as black pepper and as stinging as bog nettles, had emanated from those birds. No—had *powered* them. He'd fought it but it had constrained him, feeling like bonds of strong metal, similar to what those flying creatures themselves were made from, tightening about him. It had been no surprise that he'd lost his shifted form and shrunk back to his other, and now a headache loomed in the corners of his mind, wanting to take center stage.

Luckily, the amount of magic here didn't register as being as heavy as it had in the heart of the capital and especially at the palace. It didn't feel as thick, or as stifling. And it was good that Jagger didn't seem to be a dedicated magic user, like some elves could be. He gave the impression of being more of a dilettante about it.

All of that was interesting to ponder, as his body swung and rocked with the running water, but didn't answer any questions. Maybe their urgent need to escape had enabled him to switch to his wyvern form and take to the air? And he could have bumped into a pocket of magic on high that had short-circuited him? The silence hung heavy.

"Do you swim a lot?" he asked, trying to think of the social talk his mother would make. He got a glare back from underneath a lock of wet hair for his trouble. "I know, I know, you're a busy palace council worker." One who made time to go deflowering virgins.

"*Councilor!* Busy being a councilor!" Jagger snapped, and sneezed.

Was he trembling a bit too? Even though the river was doing all the work, keeping buoyant and one's head out of the water took effort, as did steering around floating obstacles. A large chunk of bobbing wood caught Brick's attention, and he made a grab for it. His weight overturned it, revealing it to be a log, a hollowed-out tree trunk.

"Here," he called, and snatched at Jagger's coat as he drifted past. "A boat! Sort of."

Getting up onto it proved to be more difficult than he'd imagined. Every time he got a knee or an arm on the half-trunk, it tipped over, expelling him. "A little help?" he asked, and Jagger sloshed himself to the far end. "On three?" Brick mimed pressing on the log and vaulting up. "One, two—"

"Three," they finished together, both heaving themselves aboard, and the two of them pushing down together kept their makeshift craft stable enough for them to clamber on.

"Good thinking," Jagger said.

"Much better," Brick agreed, settling as best he could in the scooped out middle. There wasn't much room, meaning they had to huddle close. "Don't suppose you stole any more fruit in the market, by any chance? I wouldn't say no to another pera."

Jagger shot him a sidelong glance but rummaged for a cloth-wrapped lump that Brick untwisted to find a hunk of the koza cheese they'd eaten last night.

"Oh, yes!" he exclaimed in joy, stuffing his face. "What?"

Jagger was smirking. "That shout sounds familiar."

Yeah, he recalled making the same exclamation, repeatedly, when Jagger had been fucking him. He shrugged and held the remains of the cheese to Jagger's lips. Jagger opened his mouth and tongued Brick's fingers as he took the morsel of cheese in. He swallowed the food and sucked Brick's digits into his mouth then stopped.

"What are we doing?" he asked.

"Oh." Brick caught up to the fact that they'd been indulging in foreplay. In a barely there boat on a rushing river, one that was bearing them into a scary forest. "I'm about to kiss you?" he said hopefully. "We could pull over to the bank..." He cast wild looks left and right, and up ahead. "What's that?"

Jagger peered then studied the flow of the water. "There are weirs, in the Welling. I suppose that must be one. Yes, it is. Oh… You mean on top of it."

"*Lying* on top of it. Looks like…" Brick squinted, but the figure became easier to see as the river pulled them nearer. "It's a man! Did you order ahead?"

"Ha ha."

"Or maybe someone else is after you?" Brick asked. His jaw dropped. "That's one beautiful man."

"Thanks." Jagger sounded sour.

"Oh, don't worry—you're a looker," Brick told him. "Good body, all that wiry muscle and a pretty face. I like your long curly hair too." He ran his fingers through it. Again. "And I might have mentioned the facial hair?"

"A few times." Jagger sounded distracted, as well he might, because it wasn't just one attractive man, slim-bodied and long-limbed, lying across the top of the weir—which was strange enough—but a few more, lying in the water, as though it were their bed. And all of them nude. If Jagger had ordered ahead, he'd gone for the buffet option.

They weren't dead, or unconscious, which Brick had feared. They were moving, stroking their long blond hair and lithe bodies. "Water fairies!" he exclaimed. "There were lots of different fairies back at the palace, for the event, and they're all sweet and pretty."

"I don't know…" Jagger replied slowly.

The one on top of the spillway sat up, swinging his long legs over to dabble his feet in the rushing water. He jumped down into it and waded in their direction. He didn't look as beautiful as Brick had thought.

"My friend Flad..." Brick swallowed and started again. "You don't know him. He's a drinking bro of mine. He thinks he's so funny. Well, he kind of is."

"Brick—"

"He performs at the Golden Claw sometimes." Brick ignored Jagger. He chuckled. "When he met the First Lady, Cerise—my mother—she asked him, 'How do you do?' all regal, like that, and he replied, 'Depends on what you're asking about,' and winked. She didn't get it."

"I don't think I do. Is there a point to this?" Jagger asked.

"I ramble when I'm nervous, okay?" Brick nodded at the man approaching. "I just wanted to say that Flad has a term for blonds who don't look as nice when you get close as they did from a distance. He calls them 'golden deceivers'."

Because this group was downright ugly. Their eyes were black, irises included, and their teeth jagged points in their chalk-white faces, while their long fingers ended in hooked claws. No longer lying playfully in the water, they stalked toward him and Jagger. The leader reached them and shot out a hand to rock their boat, his mouth open and a hissing sound coming out from between his sharp teeth.

"Hey! Stop that!" Brick shouted, grabbing at the sides of the craft. "You'll have us over."

"I think that's the idea," Jagger said. "I also think they're Morgens."

"Water spiritssss...?" Brick's last word ended in a splash and gurgle when he was tipped into the water. "That drown men!" he added, popping up.

"To make more." Jagger swiveled, trying to keep the whole group in his sights. "They're immortal."

"So I bet they get bored with one another. But that's no excuse for killing to make more companions," Brick told them.

The group struck, suddenly, swiftly, two Morgen leaping for him and two for Jagger, pulling them under in a second. Brick struggled against the four deadly hands holding him down, hating that being beneath the water robbed his movements of speed and force. Bubbles streamed from his mouth as he thrashed, and the Morgens' long hair waved like weed. He wrenched free and got his head above the surface, gulping in air, but a fifth Morgen jumped from a tree branch and landed on him, taking him down and holding on to his entire body, rolling him over and over.

"Jagger?" Brick tried to call, seeing a struggling, shaking mass to his left. The glint of a metal sword told him it was Jagger. Brick heaved and hurled himself to the melee, dragging his own attackers with him. Jagger's movements were slowing, and Brick reached for him, knowing he couldn't get there in time, couldn't help…until his wings carried him across the distance in a second.

He was shifting? Maybe partly, and enough to scare off the water bastards trying to kill him. He wrapped a wing around Jagger, snarling and jabbing his beak at the Morgens who had been holding him and who now backed away, their black eyes huge in their alarmed faces. Shoving against the water pressure, Brick broke the surface, other-form again, and yanked Jagger clear too.

"*Huuurng!*" came from both of them, the sound of four lungs snatching at air.

"And stay there!" Brick warned the huddle of long-haired, murder-hearted men on one bank. "We have to get away."

"Duh." Jagger stood and turned to the dam. "This way. Come on." He grabbed Brick's hand.

"I have got to stop doing this!" Brick yelled, jumping after Jagger again, down the short cascade of water into a lower level of the river. "Oh. That wasn't too bad. But let's make for dry land?" As they scrambled out, he realized they were still holding hands and dropped Jagger's.

He couldn't see over the weir from where they were, but the Morgen were nowhere in sight. "Maybe they have to stay on that stretch," he said. "Like, they have demarcated areas? And that's why there weren't many of them, because not many people come here?"

"Who fucking cares!" Jagger yelled. "Let's get to that clearing and make a fire. And don't take this the wrong way, but I'm wishing you were a dragon about now…" He mimed billowing flames from his nose.

"You don't want to know what *I'm* wishing," Brick replied. He was cold and shivering too and the pain threatening his skull dug in a little deeper. The forest looked half-dead to him, the trees and bushes dry.

Jagger had a fire going in a few minutes, however, and forked sticks stuck in the ground all around it to dry their clothes. "Not bad. How did a palace parchment pusher learn this?" Brick teased.

"I fuck a lot of woodland fairies." Jagger, stripping, raised an eyebrow. "Enjoying yourself? Want me to hum some sleazy music?"

Brick was staring at him.

Jagger was worth looking at—slim, strong, corded muscles, curly hair to his shoulders, gleaming brown eyes. Brick squelched out of his soggy clothes, wondering if Jagger thought he was worth the price of admission too. He reached to settle his jacket better on its improvised hanger, and his hand brushed against Jagger's shoulder. Jagger's shiver had nothing to do with the chill or damp, not by the way he looked Brick up and down and mostly in the middle and licked his lips.

"Look." He stepped nearer to Brick. "We're companions on this, well, quest, right? So how about we agree to be companions with benefits?"

Casual sex. Brick liked it—loved it—but wanted more with Jagger. *Wait. What?* "I do like fucking you," he answered, closing the gap between their bodies.

"I like fucking you." The way Jagger said it wasn't a polite mutual compliment, but a challenge. His eyes gleamed. "In fact, I want my cock in your ass. So do we have a problem? Because I have a solution."

Which was him using his hands on Brick's upper arms, and his foot behind Brick's knee to take him down, where, as soon as Brick's ass hit the grass, Jagger was on him. The arousal crackling through Brick had his body tightening in a very different way to how he felt in proximity to magic. Sex, even the prospect of it, was a kind of magic all of its own, he supposed.

Jagger swiveled his hips, rubbing his filling cock on top of Brick's already erect one. "Submit?"

Happily. Eagerly. His balls were full, and his ass was ready. The flames from the fire roared higher, mirroring how Brick felt. They burned bright red, flickering and took on a shape. As he watched, they turned yellow.

"The fire…" Jagger twisted off Brick and sat up. "It's—"

"Green. It was red, then yellow and now green. Green for go." Brick stood. "Something's coming, isn't it?"

Chapter Twelve

"Something might, given half a chance!" Jagger yelled, hurling himself to his feet and cupping his painfully full balls. "What the hell is this, National Cock Block Day? I thought the kingdom would be all juiced up, with the royal nuptials, people getting it on everywhere, but it's like the world, or fate, or what the seven stinking hells ever, is conspiring against us, when all I want is a fuck!"

"Maybe if you hadn't been so intent on fucking, that Mallon guy might not have sent more thugs after you!" Brick shouted back.

"What?" Jagger backed away from the fire. He'd set it in a dip and ringed it with big stones, but it was flaming high, as if the pit couldn't contain it. "You think this—whatever it is—is because of me? Oh, you're blameless, I suppose? A sweet little hatchling, all downy feathers and soft talons?"

"If that's what cranks your shaft…" Brick grabbed for his clothes.

Jagger shook his head. He'd told Brick the truth—he might like indulging elf-curious bed partners, but helping innocents get their freak on *really* wasn't what he was into. He liked his partners experienced, adventurous and a little on the dirty side. *Like Brick.*

And yes, I do like Brick. He liked Brick just fine the way he was, all broad shoulders and deep chest and hard…muscle. The fire, now normal flame colors again, was easing its way between two of the stones that made the perimeter of its pit, as if it had tested the barrier and found this weak spot. He pulled on his breeches, taking care over his erection.

"What if this is for both of us?" he said. "As in, someone wants us both back at the palace?"

"And there's a bounty on our…" Brick, his sexy body mostly clothed, slowed as he obviously thought of something.

Jagger wished the ring of fire would slow down too, rather than tickle out along the ground, making an arc to their left—the edges of the flames blue now. "What?" he prompted Brick.

"Bounty hunters." Brick's voice was hushed. "Fire and Brimstone. Have you heard of them?"

Jagger scoffed. Of course he had, just like he had the Flaming Arrow, who lived in 'the forest'—which one was never specified—and stole from the rich to give to the poor, or the Midnight Horses, who came into the town at night to 'clear the streets'.

Fine, so the latter existed, in the form of night soil men who came and carted off the elf waste to spread as manure on the farms…and was used by parents to convince their children they should be home at a reasonable hour. But the legendary duo who always got their quarry, Fire and Brim—

"Dear gods." Jagger wafted his hand in front of his nose. "What *is* that stench? Like rotting eggs floating in runny troll shit?"

"Sorry," Brick muttered, looking anywhere but at him.

"Why are *you* sorry about the smell of sul…fur…?" His question died away. *Sulfur. As in brimstone.* He whirled around to see the flames had almost encircled them. *Flames. As in fire. Add the two together and* – "Fire and Brimstone!" he hissed, pointing.

"And I thought I was the slow one," Brick said, ripping his jacket in his haste to don the wet garment.

Jagger grabbed his boots, stamping into them and wincing at the squelch. He slapped his forehead. "Oh, of course. Brick, fly! Shift first, obviously, and… No?"

Brick was shaking his head. "I can't. Not here. I was just trying."

"Over there, then?" Jagger suggested hopefully, while there was still a gap in the ring of fire almost enclosing them.

"Not in this place. The forest, I mean." Brick's gaze rested on the fire too, and flames reflected in his yellow irises. "It's full of magic and that dampens my ability. I have a sensitivity."

"A what?"

"An allergy," Brick muttered under his breath.

"An…" Jagger gulped and didn't look at the fire, now high and whose spiky blue tips were mirrored in the smoke rising above it, like ashy frosting. "*Allergy.*" He fought to keep calm. "To magic." He fought harder. "You couldn't be ordinary and just be allergic to flannon fruit or kholnfish. *Nooo.*" He'd lost the fight.

The ring of fire was not just a complete circle, penning them in, but was getting smaller, encroaching on them. "And we just had so much water!" he lamented. A sound like that very thing had him whipping round to Brick. "Are you… Gods in a bottle, you are! You're *pissing* on it!"

"Them. Yes." Brick finished spraying the section near him and shook a few last straw-colored drops from his dick. "Can you try? Don't tell me you're a nervous pisser, who can't go when anyone's watching?"

The flames did tamp down, where his flow had soaked them, but sprang up again when his urine stream ceased. "*Them,*" Brick had said, and Jagger saw Brimstone now, forming the inner ring imprisoning them. He glowed yellow with a white edge, to complement Fire's orange hue with its blue outline.

"You fucking disgusting vermin. Gonna enjoy taking you in." Brimstone's voice was a croak, and the fire behind him rose and flickered with his words, smoke belching. Brimstone seemed to be the leader, the brains of the duo.

The ring of flames was pressing tight round them now, the smell of smoke and sulfur overpowering. There was barely room for Jagger and Brick inside it, and once again they were forced back to back. *This pair of hunters must be even more expensive to hire than the stymph birds.*

Had Mallon really been that angered by Jagger sleeping with his son? He must have had a good match lined up for Laefe, one that would have brought in enough dowry or business to offset the prices these mercenaries must charge. The youngster hadn't mentioned it. Well, he'd had his mouth full a lot of the time, what with Jagger teaching him how to suck cock.

Jagger forced himself to think, to remember classes he'd taken in Elementary Physical-Chemistry and the magic he knew.

"My Lords…" He forced suppliance into his tone to address the bounty hunters. "It's clear you have defeated us." At his back, Brick started a little, and Jagger rubbed against him, trying to alert him. "In your, well, bounty, let us finish dressing first? We beseech thee."

Silence, broken only by the crackle and sizzle of flame, reigned for a few seconds, the two hunters conferring, perhaps.

"Fine," crackled Brimstone.

A gap appeared in the circle of fire, one wide enough for Jagger to half-step through, swing his coat free of the branch it was drying on, and pull it on, his snatchel still looped across it, meaning it accompanied him back into the fire. He sneaked his hand into his bag, feeling with his fingers and making his eyes flash a warning at Brick to say nothing…even when he eased a twist of impermeable parchment out from his snatchel.

"Take that!" he cried, undoing with a roll of his fingers the leather cord that kept the parchment bag closed and flinging the bag up high into the air in the middle of the circle. He didn't think he needed to explain to Brick what the substance was—it was obvious enough when the grains of salt started falling…and especially when they caused the flames they landed on to sputter and sink.

"That's not enough!" Brick exclaimed at the light scattering.

"It will be with this neggib herb." Well, Jagger hoped so. He blew a palmful of the dried, dusty brown flakes up too and added a slight charm for good measure. He'd never had to use any sort of size enhancement himself, but well, one never knew when it might be handy. Like now, with the salt growing from a dusting to an avalanche, making the fire splutter to nothing.

He covered his ears at the shrieks Brimstone made. Oh no, that must have been Fire, because Jagger had to pinch his nose against the rotting stench Brimstone emitted when extinguished. "Dung in a bucket—it's like it farted itself to death," he observed, wafting the air, half-choked and his eyes watering enough to put out any blaze. "At least we're dry." He was a goblet half-full sort of elf. "You can thank me later. And I know what form I want the thanks to take. Brick? They're gone…are you okay?"

Stupid. He clearly wasn't, not sunk to his knees, rocking back and forth like that. His fingers splayed around his head and his knuckles were white with pressing inward, as though he were trying to squeeze out the pain attacking him from within.

"Hey. Hey there." Jager bent and gathered what he could of Brick to him, holding him close. He rocked with him, resting a hand between his shoulder blades and muttering soothing words. Should he try a charm? He started to wrack his brains, to think what would be the next move when he caught Brick peeping up at him, just his eye visible. Well, one golden eye and a raised eyebrow.

"Magic? You're thinking of trying more magic when that's *what's left me like this?"*

Jagger heard it as though Brick had spoken the words. "Sorry. I'm the slow and the stupid one," he murmured, feeling the slight chuckle his still-kneeling companion gave at that. After a minute, Brick straightened, his eyes still closed, and Jagger sank to his own knees next to him. Slowly, not wanting his touch to startle Brick, he drew close and rubbed Brick's temples.

Jomb's body servant attended to him like that, stroking tiny circles with a cloth soaked in a lemonherb and feverfew infusion when Jomb had been poring over documents for too long and strained himself. It stank out the council room, but Jagger would be grateful for a vial of the mixture now. Oh, but Brick must have his own stuff!

"Where's your medication, for your alle—sensitivity?" he asked.

Brick opened his eyes and caught his wrists, bringing his hands down. "In my stomach. I took it all."

And then more magic happened. Jagger felt guilty. Brick had explained about his condition, even though it had pained him, no pun intended, to reveal a weakness, and Jagger had gone and done the very thing that acerbated it.

"Okay, so we need more." Jagger looked around as if an apothecary had sprung up, its small serving-window shutters rattling open for business. It hadn't. They weren't. "We have to get the stuff you need, I mean," he amended. "What do you take?"

"I don't need it back home. My mother doles it out to me when we travel or have magic-user or magic-imbued visitors who bring it on." Brick got to his feet, a little unsteadily, but he managed, and only swayed once. "She's mentioned devil's claw, I think?"

"Sure that isn't what the servants call her, behind her back?" Jagger couldn't resist quipping.

Brick laughed, gritting his teeth and wincing. "No, that'd be Catija. Her name."

Jagger realized how little he knew about wyverns. "Calling her by her name pisses her off, how?"

"Oh, her married-in name's Cerise. When she joined the Ruby Throne."

And he knew next to nothing about royal wyverns. For the first time it struck him that Brick must be a prince, or their equivalent. But first and foremost, he was a person in pain, and Jagger wanted that dealt with. "Well, I don't know what dragon's claw is—"

"Devil's claw," Brick corrected.

"Or that. But here we use gesic root for anything from head pain to allergic reactions so..."

"Oh." Brick nodded. "The page brought me some last night, I think. At least, the name sounds familiar. A drink that was smoking."

"Let's leave the subject of smoke and fire, shall we?" Jagger settled Brick's jacket properly on him. "A hard as that is seeing how we both reek of it." He took a sniff of his hair. It could do with a wash, but he didn't feel like bathing in a stream, not after the Welling River. "Gesic root grows in the moss of ash trees, and I bet there's ash trees a bit farther in the forest. Come on."

Brick was still quiet as they set off, and Jagger asked him to tell him about the Ruby Throne, to give him something to think about. And because he was interested. They walked, munching on the last of the fruit—juicy, fuzzy-skinned perzics—Jagger had, Brick describing the wyvern kingdom and its ways. The moon rose, casting wavering shadows of the tall oak trees and making night scents bloom, their perfume muffling the acrid smoke and sharp sulfur of their last battle.

"Looks like a clearing just there." Jagger found he was reluctant to break the silence that had fallen between him and Brick. It had been comfortable, companionable, them holding hands without a thought. *Well, we are companions with benefits.* His skin tingled with arousal— *No. Awareness.* He whipped round, but could see nothing, not even a night bird in the trees.

"Call me crazy," Brick started, and Jagger bit back any witticism. "But do you think we're being watched?"

Something rustled. *Wind. In the trees.*

"But that it's okay?" Brick continued.

"Oddly, yes." Jagger had no objection to an audience. What could there be here? Fauna and— *Oh. Right.* He swallowed. "I've remembered something about the Forbidden Forest. Like, how it got its name?"

"Which is because…?"

Brick jerked his chin at the grove they'd just walked into. "It's home to dryads and hamadryads."

"Ah."

Chapter Thirteen

"We don't have those back home," Brick said, "but it must be like meeting with any spirit, right?"

"Riiiight?"

"Like, when you meet a ghost, be polite to it?" Seeing Jagger didn't understand, Brick mimed meeting a dead spirit, all outstretched arms and *whooo* noises, and treating it with deference. "That respect and acknowledgment is what they want. What they're hanging around for." He looked around the moonlit glade they stood in. It would have been prettier if the trees and bush hadn't looked so dry.

"Dear forest spirits," Jagger began. "Please may we have some medicine for pain or to deal with sensitivity to magic? Thank you."

The trees whispered in response. Well, their leaves rustled, rubbing together, but nothing happened.

"Don't you find this forest, and this clearing, a little arid?" Brick muttered, his hand over his mouth like his family did when saying anything personal in public.

"Dryer than a troll's pubic hair," Jagger agreed.

And stuffed with magic. Brick's veins buzzed with it.

"Well, no one's appeared with meds." Jagger shrugged. "I'll light up a torch and we can go hunting for gesic root."

"No." Brick put a hand on his arm. "We can't just take. With spirits, you don't get without giving." Cerise would be happy that all her 'protocol for other species' lessons had paid off.

"What do they want?" Jagger asked.

Brick rubbed a dry frond between his finger and thumb, careful not to crush it. It released a hint of a heady scent, one he could imagine would make his head swim, if the plant was at full strength. "Liquid," he answered.

"Rain, you mean?"

"No, it rains here. Maybe it's because the tree canopy is so dense that raindrops can't penetrate? It needs something closer. Nearer. *Owww!*" He hopped where Jagger had trodden on his foot. "Why did you do that?" He dashed a tear of pain from his eye.

"That's why." Jagger pointed where Brick flicked the teardrop to the ground.

Elves can be so smug. Brick was almost pleased that nothing changed. He could imagine Jagger doing a dance of triumph. "It didn't do anything. Let's try you." He pushed back his sleeves, pretending he was getting ready to thump Jagger and make *him* cry. "Elf tears are special, aren't they?" He frowned, trying to recall that bit of lore Cerise must have imparted at some point. "What is it they do, or can do?"

"Nothing. And nothing." Jagger gave him a sidelong look. "Blood holds a lot of power, of course, so we should keep that as a last resort. But what about cum?"

"Cum. You…want me to jerk off? In a glade, in the moonlight?"

"While that sounds poetic, no." Jagger threw back his hair and reached out to cradle the side of Brick's neck. He stroked with his thumb, and Brick's pulse kicked up at the touch. "I mean I'm feeling horny."

Midway through his eye roll in response, Brick noticed their shadows cast on the ground. They were elongated, as he'd expected…but his was two-legged and long-necked, with wings, his wyvern form. *That* he hadn't expected. "Everything makes you horny," he finally replied. He rubbed his head into the back of Jagger's hand on his neck, more like a cat than a wyvern at that moment. He was about to kiss, about to fuck, a sexy elf, one he was drawn to but felt guilty at possibly tying to him—he had weightier things to think about than his shadow.

"Me too," he said, when Jagger hesitated, perhaps recalling Brick had been sick just recently. He felt good now though. "I'll even let you fuck me."

"*Even let me*?" Jagger scoffed. "Be *begging* me. Again."

"Fair point," Brick had to admit. "Yeah, I did. Just like you did me."

"Oh, I *did* you all right." Jagger's grin was carnal. "And so…"

As if a referee had called "Go," they raced to undress, and Brick had barely finished before Jagger had him flat on his back, their discarded clothes cushioning him from the ground.

"You know, I feel you don't get enough praise," came indistinctly from where Jagger was nipping at Brick's collarbone.

"I do." Brick thought of the 'build Brick up' compliments he got for carrying out the busy work designed for him.

"Fine. Admiration then." Jagger reached his nipple and began his worship. His voice sounded even more muffled as he promised, "So I'm going to tell you how I feel about each bit of you. Or if not tell you, show you."

Brick wanted to tell Jagger something—that he'd never been this aroused, with any other partner before, but it was hard to speak when Jagger was using one hand to toy with his nipple ring and the other to cup his ass cheek. Not to mention he was astride Brick, squeezing his waist with his knees. Lust shot through Brick like a dram of fire whiskey. His nipples peaked and stung, and he loved it. He wished he could see the darker shade Jagger's sucking had left them. Maybe an old rose color, he thought, almost coming at the twinges of good-pain.

"I like biting my way down your body," he heard from his navel, Jagger having worked his way lower, to kneel between Brick's legs. Brick didn't recall having spread them. "So soft here…"

Brick bellowed through his nose when Jagger nipped his stomach, next to his belly button, then arched like a bow when Jagger slid the hand that had been tugging on his nipple ring to his dick. Brick rutted a little, rubbing his cock on whatever part of Jagger it came into contact with, then barely held in a shriek when Jagger licked into the hollow of his navel. "No one's ever… Didn't know that was so sensitive," he said, his body already thrashing.

Sweat beaded his skin, which Jagger licked off as soon as it formed. Brick's cock pulsed and twitched in

Jagger's fairly loose grasp—he wasn't working it, wasn't pulling it—and Brick thought he might come, just from that. That would be fine. Jagger would have him hard again.

"Gonna take you in my mouth." Jagger sat back a little and looked him in the eyes. "Do you know what a challenge you are? Not just the size, but all those fucking amazing bands…that swell? I didn't think I'd be able to get my mouth around you when I first saw you."

He managed now, though, bending low to bob his head over Brick, first flickering his tongue then delivering that wet, hot, just-right suction that had thrilled Brick to the core yesterday in the tavern. Now, he was fairly certain he was rutting on Jagger's shoulder.

"Love how wyverns moan," Jagger paused long enough to say. "Or is it just you?"

He'd better not conduct any comparison surveys to find out. Brick's possessiveness over the elf stunned him. They'd barely met and Jagger…was draping Brick's legs over his shoulders.

"Want in." Jagger caressed Brick's ass to show him. "Don't worry—I'll keep you in my mouth."

"No." Brick brought his legs down. He wanted a taste too, and it had to be soon, before Jagger had him coming, because now he wanted to bring Jagger off in his mouth as well. *No, not as well—first.* The need to have Jagger gasping and shooting his cum down Brick's throat burned in him. He hated losing contact with Jagger's mouth, even for the few seconds it took him to lie alongside him, facing the way that would let them suck each other at the same time. As soon as he could, he tugged Jager's cock to him and nuzzled into his springy hair before he sucked the head, then took the length deep.

The next second, he had to pull off—whatever Jagger was doing to his dick had it tingling. The feel was stronger than speared-mint—than peppered-mint, even—and made him gasp. And glow. And grin. And dive back onto Jagger's cock, cradling his balls and taking his taste for his own. Jagger's flavor, something between spice and smoke, earth and wild, was addictive, and Brick was happy getting his fix. Happy, too, to thrust into Jagger's mouth, then pull out to the tip, so Jagger chased his dick with his tongue that was almost as clever as a wyvern's, before shoving deep again.

He cast a glance to the side of him, seeking out his shadow, curious to see if it were still his wyvern shape, as he'd glimpsed it before. *No.* This time, the black facsimiles of *two* winged creatures met his eye. They rose and moved just as he and Jagger did, meaning the shadows were theirs…and both of them in wyvern form.

Only for a minute though—even as Brick watched, the shadows became those of two men, both with slightly pointed-tipped ears. So, two elven men. Jagger was an elven male, obviously, but Brick…wasn't. What did it mean? He didn't know, any more than he understood why Jagger had seemed at the tavern to have wyvern body parts—including the banded cock that so fascinated him and that Brick shouldn't have had in other-form. But it did give him an idea. A wicked, unheard-of idea…

He curled into himself, then kneeled, smiling at the needy whine his withdrawal made his partner give. "Turn over. On your hands and knees." He slapped at

Jagger's ass to get him in position, harder than he'd meant to, but he was heavy-handed, and the thwack was meaty. The noise Jagger made at getting a spank… It took Brick a second to catch on. The elf could dish it out but clearly didn't find many partners who served it up to him.

"You like that," he said, curling over Jagger where he knelt on all fours, and slapping his ass again, to test his theory.

"I do." Jagger sounded happy at the discovery. He waggled his rear for Brick. "I'm up for a game of naughty elf punished by big bad wyvern shifter anytime," he purred.

"I don't think this is exactly punishment…" Brick grabbed both Jagger's cheeks then bent his head and ran his tongue down his cleft. When he reached Jagger's hole, he had to hold him steady—he was already writhing. It didn't take much laving to get Jagger soft, and Brick didn't need him very pliable, just enough for him to insinuate his tongue tip inside his loosened pucker. *The forked tip of his elongated shifted-form tongue.*

Brick had part-shifted back in the tavern, without meaning to, without understanding. Now, he did it simply by thinking about it, as naturally as the day taking over from the night, as if he'd done it many times before. He hadn't though and hadn't even known it was possible.

He wriggled in past the first ring of muscles, and Jagger went wild, clutching at the grass beneath him, tearing out big handfuls and clawing at the earth. His shouts and cries rang from the treetops.

Brick grinned, wondering if Jagger could feel his widened mouth in his crack too. His grin was at the thought that his partner was about to discover that a wyvern's tongue wasn't just incredibly long, slim, yet strong and flexible enough to seek out places inside a man's ass that had him gasping. It was also deft enough to use the bifurcation at its tip like the deadliest missile, snaking it to flick over and caress that spot deep inside that had a grown elf weeping. And that they were dimpled, possessing small groups of tiny, raised bumps here and there.

Yep, the scream Jagger gave, followed by the stream of babbled syllables Brick didn't think was even a real language said he felt those raised dots on his inner muscles and sensitive walls.

The length of a wyvern's tongue meant Brick's face wasn't buried in Jagger's ass when he penetrated him with it—despite Jagger trying to thrust back into him—and Brick stared at the sight of Jagger's pucker contracting around his tongue. The sight was the most perfect visual parallel to the sensations he felt, the pulsations of Jagger's muscles gripping and releasing him—involuntary actions that sent ripples along his tongue as Brick fucked Jagger with it.

He'd intended to open Jagger up to fuck him but knew he wouldn't last. He sneaked a hand around Jagger's hip to his cock and gripped it—with a wyvern-form paw. Well, not so much the rough pads, but the long, taloned claws. It was dangerous and dirty and overwhelmed Brick too.

Jagger's cock swelled and he arched, clamping down hard on Brick's tongue and screaming his pleasure as he came, his cum spurting out from between Brick's talons to the forest floor. The convulsions of his body dislodged Brick free. He withdrew his tongue and pressed close, losing himself in the throes of his release, a climax that felt like a lightning bolt had struck his soul.

His shout, as he rubbed on Jagger's ass, was deeper than Jagger's scream, but just as loud, and his release as copious, fountaining from his cock to cover Jagger's ass and lower back and drip from his flesh. And still he kept coming, like never before. He'd never felt anything like this ecstasy. This connection. It blurred his vision and dulled his hearing.

Jagger's arms must have given out—he collapsed, sliding his spent cock from Brick's hand. And it was a hand now, with fingers and not claws. Just as Brick wondered if Jagger had seen it—*hells, if it actually happened*—Jagger heaved himself over onto his back and stared from Brick's hand to his mouth, then to Brick's face.

It was real and he saw. Okay.

Jagger rubbed his throat. It must be sore. Brick's was, and he and Jagger were sweating and shivering, their cocks sticky. The night around them had grown bright, luminescent, everything standing out sharply as though lit by candles. Brick opened his mouth to speak, but before he could utter a syllable, the rustling of the leaves—no, the trees themselves—intensified, growing so loud that Brick covered his ears.

Shadows thickened around the tree trunks, wavering so it looked like the trees were moving. But they weren't. The blurs and flickers were forms emerging from the trunks, some slipping through like smoke pouring though chinks and some pulling themselves free with seeming difficulty.

"Dryads." Jagger nudged him to look, and wherever Brick's gaze landed, there were more, ethereal, insubstantial and plentiful.

"And hamadryads," Brick agreed, then frowned. "What's the difference?"

"Never ask that!" Jagger groaned. "It's one of those things you just don't ask or know."

Typical me. But if he had wanted to ask, now would be a good time.

Because they all began to converge…

Chapter Fourteen

"What do you call this?" Jagger whispered when he was able to speak. He tracked another group of tree beings as they converged on one another in a chorus of sighs and gasps, which, almost more quickly than his ears could keep up with, became shouts and cries.

"Elf porn?" Brick replied, his gaze pinned on a group to their left.

"They're not elves."

"I meant porn *for* elves. Free porn, then?" Brick's swallow sounded almost pained in the moonlight. "I've never done that."

"A threesome?" Jagger queried. He'd judged Brick more adventurous than that.

Brick got a hand to Jagger's chin and twisted his head in the direction he was staring in.

"Oh that..." Yeah, it made the threesome look tame. "I can't even count that many," he commented.

"Are those twins?" Brick dropped his voice to ask. "With...triplets?"

"Would that make quintuplets?" Jagger had to raise his voice to ask that over the screams ringing out into the night. "I know what it makes me."

"Horny?" Brick asked on a resigned sigh, but his own…interest was stirring. He pointed high in the air, and when Jagger turned to see what he was indicating, Brick pushed him flat and was on top of him.

"So it's true—wyverns are wily," Jagger commented, hooking his legs around Brick to hold him close. He liked the wyvern's solid weight on him, and that in this position he could grind their crotches together, for a few seconds before Brick rolled and had Jagger on top. He eased his hands to Jagger's ass and fingered his crease, caressing his still soft and open pucker.

"That was *spectacular*." Jagger knew Brick would understand what he referred to. "The wyvern tongue one of your moves?" He didn't like that unfamiliar note in his voice.

"I never did it before," Brick replied, pressing in a little.

"Well, it opened me up good." Jagger wriggled.

"I've never done this before, either." Brick jerked his head to indicate the orgy taking place all around them.

"But…you want to join in?" Jagger tried to gauge Brick's mood.

Brick grinned. "I want to watch, sure. And listen."

The sounds were arousing, to say the least. Each gasped-out or bitten-off cry raised the hairs on Jagger's skin and each scream or shout of pleasure or fulfilment had his balls tightening.

"And I want to fuck you," Brick continued, thrusting up. "Nice and slow."

"Hmm." Jagger pretended to consider. "You want to watch but be inside me. So I guess that rules out missionary. Oh, you have a position in mind?"

Brick answered by tipping Jagger off, to one side of him, his back to Brick. His cock was already nudging at Jagger's hole. Jagger cast about for his bag to rummage in it and retrieve a small pot that he held up for Brick.

"Lube?" Brick took it. "Love how you brought the essentials for a journey, food and lubricant."

"Be prepared..." Jagger stretched his already relaxed body luxuriously on the grass, pillowing his chin on his folded arms and bending one leg up to expose his hole, for Brick to do just that to him.

A group of...six? seven? was busy near them. Jagger wondered if Brick was consciously timing his pushes of two thick, meaty fingers into him to replicate the pace at which the tallest tree spirit in the group was thrusting his cock down the throat of another male on his hands and knees in front of him. The volume and rhythm of the moans Jagger gave in response echoed those of the male getting sucked. The very air felt like an aphrodisiac.

Brick pulled Jagger a little more toward him, his only warning before he lined up and, in a slow, steady push, filled him to the hilt. His pace was leisurely, the movements of his hips more rolls than thrusts, and his arms around Jagger a tight band.

"*Gods.*" Jagger wished he could articulate the bliss spreading through him, perhaps emanating from where Brick's cock was piercing him, but spreading to every corner of his body and literally making his toes curl. He twisted a foot back, tangling it with Brick's ankles and digging his toenails into Brick's flesh.

Maybe Brick understood what Jagger couldn't express, because he took Jagger's hand and curled their fingers together, making Jagger's finger and thumb pinch one of his nipples. At the same time, he licked up the shell of Jagger's ear, into his elf-point, and Jagger melted. Maybe at some point in the past, at some distant stage in elf evolution, their ear tips had been the sensitive, debilitating erogenous zones that the unknowing still believed them to be today, rather than the mildly pleasant spots they were.

And sure, Jagger had enjoyed exaggerating their sensitivity for non-elf hook-ups, feigning being brought to his knees when his ear points were caressed or licked or even breathed on, if he was in the mood to play up to a stereotype, then shout "Psyche!" and startle and hopefully educate the guy.

But this, Brick giving them tiny licks and even tinier nips, so Jagger never knew when Brick's teeth would come into play, and Brick doing that at the same time he was bringing Jagger's nipples to sharp, urgent peaks *and* fucking his ass with his huge cock that any minute now could sprout those gods-be-worshipped bands? Jagger had never felt such rapture, been buffeted by so much bliss.

His ass clamped down on Brick's cock with every bite Brick took, and it made Brick grunt in response, his breath stirring even more of Jagger's senses. Brick had said he wanted to watch, and the sights just in front of them were worth viewing. "Are you looking where I am?" he whispered.

"Oh, yeah," rumbled from Brick along Jagger's chest, the sound seeming to land in his balls.

The knowledge that they were both staring into the huge, dazed eyes of the male tree spirit, who, after having sucked off one dryad so well, was now taking another's dick in his ass, his fractured cries ringing his pleasure to the sky, was dizzying. And when Jagger looked up from that spirit, the guy claiming his ass was staring at them too.

Either the tree dryad slowed, or Brick sped up a little, because their rhythms matched, right down to the speed of the hand on Jagger's dick, and the slapping sound their bodies made. But it was about more than the sex, as mind-blowing, as soul-bending as that was. Jagger felt a pull to Brick and he'd never experienced anything like that before. It was very unlike the way he lived his life…the way he *liked* his life. In fact, it tugged him in the opposite direction, and it confused the hells out of him.

There's a whole world out there to fuck! he shouted inside his head, and, as if he'd voiced the words, Brick drove his cock into Jagger's ass hard, dragging a moan from him and slamming him forward on the grass. All Jagger was sure about at the moment was that he wanted this. "Need this."

That part was out loud, and Brick slammed harder and longer than ever with a hoarse shout, his hot cum jetting deep into Jagger. That and his hand on Jagger's cock pushed Jagger over into the storm of his climax, its power tearing through him. He'd never felt anything so intense, something that touched every inch of skin on his body and every nerve within it.

Brick hugged him tighter, his breath hot on Jagger's neck. He gave a small start, and Jagger opened his eyes to see a shape coalescing alongside them—the dryad they'd been watching. He was mirroring Jagger's position, which was only fair, since Jagger and Brick had been copying him a few minutes ago…well, copying the pace and intensity at which *he'd* been taking at least two cocks.

Jagger got an impression of a shadow behind the dryad. Was there another guy lying there with him, like Brick was with Jagger? If so, was this guy's cock still in the dryad's ass, like Brick's was in his? Jagger wanted to ask Brick if he thought so too.

There was a lot he wanted to ask Brick about, and hardly any of it connected to the figure or figures lying next to them. But it would have to keep, he supposed. Brick gave him a last hug and slipped free. Jagger instantly missed him. He glanced up—if there had been another guy behind the dryad on his side next to them, he dissolved and vanished. Jagger and Brick were left only their companion in fucking, or whatever what they'd done was called.

The other dryads hadn't sneaked back into their trees, though, merely retreated to form a circle at the edge of the clearing. The air pulsed with their presence. Jagger had no need to hold his breath to see if he could hear their breathing—they were panting from their sexcapades, the air heavy with the scent of their cum. It made the atmosphere hyper-charged with arousal. It wouldn't take much for them all, Brick and him included, to start screwing again.

Brick cleared his throat, making Jagger look over his shoulder at him. He thought he could read the same questions, the same confusion in his eyes.

"We should dress," Brick said.

Was he speaking to the dryad next to them as well as Jagger? Jagger could have told him dryads had no hang-ups about nudity. And probably no clothes to put on. He nodded and stood, passing Brick various items of clothing and accepting his, and all the while the trees spirit watched them.

"Well…" Jagger tried, once he was clothed.

The guy stood too, as tall, slim and ethereal as people mistakenly believed elves to be. "What a rush!" he exclaimed, and whooped, the sound taken up by the other tree spirits. "We haven't had that energy in an *age*—we haven't left the trees in so long."

"Glad we could help?" Jagger shot a glance at Brick and saw he was at a loss too. "*Be polite,*" he reminded Brick on a fake cough. "I'm Jagger, and this is Brick."

"Ash." The dryad put his hand to his chest and bowed.

"As in the tree?" Brick asked.

"Yes. You wouldn't be able to pronounce my actual name." Ash shook back his long hair. His eyes looked a pale gray in the moonlight. "You need food and drink after that? I do."

Another dryad scurried up with fruit, using a flat stone for a platter, and a second came bearing drinks in leaf cups, that they deposited on the ground.

"Ambrosial fruit and pomeberry juice." Ash sat, gesturing that they should too.

Brick snatched a handful of the pulpy fruit and threw it into his mouth. Jagger had wondered if he were still growing, the way he needed food. *No, just has a big frame to fill. And he can fill mine anytime too.*

"The juice…" Ash started, half-turning aside.

Brick choked on the mouthful he'd taken, and Jagger thumped him on the back.

"Has to be mixed with water," Ash continued, moving his shoulder for the dryad behind him to pour sparkling water into the cups. "Or else it tastes like gall."

"See that, yep," Brick answered, his eyes streaming. "Ash, are you the potentate? The king?"

"The duly elected spokes-dryad, you mean." Ash seemed a little bit of a hippie.

Jagger took a drink of the pomeberry juice and found it heady. The expression *drunken orgy* crossed his mind. *Only, here, the participants get smashed after.* Which reminded him. "Did we pass?" he queried. "With what we gave?"

"Pass the entrance test?" Brick added.

Ash laughed, his chuckles taken up by the circle of dryads. "Oh yeah. And not that we didn't appreciate the show, but usually we just make travelers answer a riddle."

"A riddle?" Jagger echoed. "We could just have answered a gods-damned riddle?"

"Yeah, you know, like, I die once every year, but grow stronger over time—what am I?" Ash asked.

"A tree!" someone called from the shadows, following that with, "What has lots of bark, but no bite?

"A tree!" called another dryad. "What wears rings without having fingers?"

"A tree!" Ash answered. He crammed a slice of fruit into his mouth and asked around it, "What leaves without going anywhere?"

"Is it," Jagger asked, fighting not to roll his eyes, "a tree?"

"Oh, you heard that one." Ash looked from Jagger to Brick. "Rowan, ask one of your brain teasers."

"Which side of a tree has the most leaves?" called a male voice, presumably Rowan's.

"Erm..." Jagger tried to think.

"The outside!" Ash slapped his thigh. "Here's another—what looks like half a spruce tree?"

"The other half," Rowan shouted.

"Jagger..." Brick's voice was a whine and he pulled on Jagger's sleeve.

"Which animals can jump higher than a tree?" asked a new voice.

"All of them. Trees can't jump!" answered a chorus.

"Make it stop," Brick pleaded. "It's worse than hoot night at the Claw."

"Ash—" Jagger began, to be stopped by an upraised hand.

"How many oranges grow on a tree?" Ash demanded.

"Erm, all of them?" Jagger tried, and the entire clearing erupted in applause and cheers and loud whistles. "Okay. Well, we're pleased we could assist you to...'leaf' your trees..." He waited for more applause, but instead a slow hiss went up.

"I guess they do the tree jokes," Brick muttered.

Chapter Fifteen

"Spokes-dryad Ash, we're on a quest and ask your help."

"*Would* ask your help," Brick corrected Jagger, to make it more formal. "*Thy* help." Yes, that sounded even better.

"We seek out the true meaning of a prophecy," Jagger continued.

"An ancient prophecy," Brick butted in again.

"Is it? I'd never heard of it until recently." Jagger frowned.

"Me neither," Brick realized. "I guess they were keeping it from us?"

"And anyway, aren't all prophecies ancient?" Jagger asked. "If you want to get technical."

Oh, touched a nerve. A councilor-shaped nerve. Jagger must have thought he was the best at all the official stuff. "I crave your indulgence," Brick said with a slight bow. *Let him out-official that.*

"There's already been a lot of...indulgence." Ash tipped his head to one side, a sly grin tilting his lips. "But anyway, what is this foretelling?"

Jagger and Brick both started to speak at once, and Ash held up a hand. "The eldest should speak. They have less time."

"Go ahead, old man," Brick invited, patting him on the back.

Jagger made a quite a good job of explaining, Brick thought, listening carefully, and even brought out the scroll from his snatchel, to show the actual words.

"Well, I'm no soothsayer," Ash said, looking from one to another, "but it seems clear enough that the divination speaks of a union between the two houses...in the form of you two."

"No." Brick shook his head. "No one should have to be tied to m— To be tied," he corrected. "Especially Jagger." The elf was vibrant and burned brightly—to think of him forced to spend the rest of his life with Brick the Dull, Brick the Plodder and Blunderer, the shifter who'd be a permanent invalid in the elf kingdom? *It's cruel.*

Sure, Brick brought out the fun in him, and he could give free rein to those parts of himself he supressed around the official world of the Ruby Throne, but that was because he and Jagger were outside real life here, were companions with benefits. A few days of Brick farting and belching as he met Jagger's fellow councilors or nose-bleeding over dignitaries from other realms as he tried to show them what shifting looked like, and Jagger would soon lose what little patience he had with him...and all liking for him.

"Okay, so the sex is amazing, but..." *Oh, troll shit.* He'd said that out loud. "I mean, and in addition, I seek medicaments for a sensitivity. Oh, fine—an allergy. I don't deal well with magic."

"This sacred grove is imbued with much magic, and you seem fine to me," Ash observed.

"Is it the chemicals released by the amazing sex?" Jagger asked, his lips twitching as he tried to hide a smirk. "Because if so, I have the remedy to hand, one might say." He added a hip thrust.

"Or is this clearing not as magical as it once was?" Ash mused. "I do sense changes, new energies, new zephyrs. A new dawn, perhaps, with my people out of the shadows…" He shook his head slightly and looked as though he were pulling himself together. "What treatment is it you need?" He sat forward, interested.

"Gesic root," Jagger answered.

"Oh." Ash curled his lip.

Brick guessed that gesic must be a generic cure-all, real beginners' level herblore. He looked a question at Jagger, who shrugged.

"It gets the job done," he muttered.

"Take what you need from my tree, there," Ash offered, practically rolling his eyes as his fellow-dryads tsked.

"This is almost too easy," Jagger said a minute later, when they were searching the moss around the tall ash tree. "Dryads are supposed to be tricky and—"

"One caveat," Ash called across.

"You *had* to do it," Brick muttered, elbowing Jagger.

"Take what you need," Ash continued. "As in, to satisfy your immediate needs. What the forest provides is not to be hoarded away from the earth in which it grows." He brought over a fresh cup of juice, and Jagger finished tugging free a handful of gesic root.

Ash gasped and almost dropped the cup. His face flushed and his mouth gaped open.

"I think he's just come!" Brick whispered.

"Ah. I think we discovered the reason you can't go around harvesting stuff from here. There seems to be a...connection between the vegetation and the spirits," Jagger surmised.

He passed him the root, and Brick chomped on it, swallowing the mulch down with the fruit juice and water mix. Both were awful and he held his stomach with his hand, willing it not to heave.

Handing the cup back, Brick noticed a tiny flower growing near the roots. It must have been a bright pink, in daylight, but even in this light, its color and pointy petals intrigued him. He bent and, pretending he was tying his shoe, picked it. It was one of a small bunch, so he snapped them all off and slipped them into his pocket. *You never know what you'll need in a wind,* as they said back home.

"Will the effects of the herb last until we reach the Cave of the Worlds?" he asked.

"You'd best hurry." Ash seemed to commune mentally with his fellow dryads. "Take the shorter route underground." He pointed down, at the roots of his tree, and although nothing changed or moved, a hole was evident. *No, a tunnel.*

"Ah." Jagger took a quick peek down and his lips tightened. "You know, a scenic route could be more...scenic."

"You want to spend longer in your wyvern's company." Ash looked understanding.

"No, it's not that," Jagger replied.

Brick tried not to feel stabbed in the ribs. "No, not that," he parroted, unable to think of anything else to say.

"Brick, I didn't mean…" Jagger reached for his hand, but Brick crossed his arms. Jagger sighed. "I don't like confined spaces, okay?"

Oh. Brick recalled Jagger leaving by a window rather than an escape tunnel, and his heart squeezed for the elf. "I understand. Well, what if we go overland? I've had a whole lot of medicine—I could shift and fly us."

"What if you feel ill again? Or if the stymph birds are waiting for another attack? No." Jagger folded his arms too. "The shorter way's better."

"We'll get through it together, okay?" Brick promised him.

"And you would dispute this prophecy that speaks of the two of you uniting," Ash said, under his breath.

"We must take our leave." Brick closed his eyes at what he'd just said. "I wasn't— I didn't mean 'leaf'."

"And I give thee gifts for thy journey." Ignoring Brick's babble, Ash stood straight. A fat stick appeared in his hand and he handed it over. "A quarter staff," he explained.

"Because…?" Brick asked.

"I can manifest objects made of wood that you might need on your journey." Ash shrugged.

"Could we trade this for a javelin, in that case?" Jagger asked. "More useful."

"If it's no trouble," Brick added, elbowing Jagger.

"My thanks." Jagger took the pointed spear Ash had changed the staff into and slotted it into his sword belt. "Oh, and anything else wooden you think might come in handy…" Jagger frowned at the stringed instrument in Ash's hands. "Thank you."

He handed it to Brick with a slight shrug.

Well, he did say dryads were tricky. He helped Jagger onto the small steps descending into the earth and followed him down.

"Go right at the Great Cavern," Ash called after them. "Oh, and beware the Lord of All Roots, also known as the Taproot, and you'll be fine."

"The Taproot?" Brick thought he must have misheard.

"Yeah, he'll want to encase you in his snare and keep you down there forever. Just remember you're in his realm and give him his due," floated down to him before the hole they'd climbed through sealed itself up above them.

Brick didn't know if Jagger had heard the dryad's parting words and decided not to ask him. Tiny white-green lights stuck into the earthen walls shone and lit up the short flight of steps and the mud-and-stone-smelling passage they led down to. He was glad this tunnel was short—it was hard to walk along it like some hunched, bent insect.

"This must be the Great Cavern Ash mentioned," he said, at the huge space that opened up before them and stretched all around them. Glowing chunks of rock lit it up a little. His foot crunched on something. A small bone. There were more.

"That suggests habitation—they're trodden down," Jagger said. "Did…you hear something?"

"Like…?"

"What lives in caves?" Jagger asked.

Trolls, Brick tried not to think. *Think of sweet little animals instead.* But any cuddly thing he envisioned turned into rock rats and cave bats, all pointy claws, even pointier teeth and scabby fur. He shuddered.

"Let's go. Oh, I'm not scared," he assured Jagger. "I just think we should hurry. Come on."

"Go right," Ash had said. It was a small gap and Brick went first, bending a little and hoping his ass distracted Jagger. It led to a waterway of some sort, narrow, with barely enough space for them to stand against the wall without their feet dipping into the spring that ran down the middle of the tunnel.

"There's a fair being held as part of the wedding celebrations, isn't there?" Brick asked. "What's your favorite ride or game?"

Jagger eyed him. "Are you babbling?"

"A bit," Brick admitted. "Personally, I never like the ones where you sit in a carved-out log and it rushes along a track that zigs and zags, then splashes into a pool of water at the bottom, you know?"

"And you're mentioning this because…?"

"Because there's a boat tied up to that rock there." He inched around to examine what turned out to be a flat-bottomed boat. "It looks sound." He scrutinized the craft further. "It's even got paddles."

"Paddles? Well, that settles it—we'll jump straight in." Jagger threw up his hands.

"And that's you being snarky." Brick took another look around. "You see another solution?"

"No." Jagger climbed aboard. "Happy now?"

"Not particularly," Brick answered. "And you're still being a jerk, in case you didn't know?"

He slipped the rope free and held the craft steady enough for them to step in. Jagger took the far seat, leaving the one facing the direction they were heading in for Brick, and heaped their possessions in the middle, between the seats.

Brick pushed the boat from the side and the water carried it, and them away. Soon, the waterway widened, and the walls and roof glowed with more lights, white and occasionally rose-pink, illuminating their journey. Colored gleams shone in the water too, maybe phosphorus fishes.

It was almost dreamlike, with the swish of the water and the gentle motion of the boat relaxing, nothing like their wilder ride down the Welling River. Jagger took the wooden instrument Ash had given them. It looked like a guitara, with twelve strings set into two rows of six, and he plucked them, tentatively at first, then tried a few major, then some minor chords.

"You play?" Brick asked, amazed.

"I learned," Jagger corrected, his lips lifting in a wry smile. "But with me being so ancient, it was many moons ago."

"Oh, you play all right!" Brick told him a minute or two later, listening to the tune Jagger plucked from the instrument. It was mournful with a sense of loss and feel of resignation to fate shot through it, and Brick couldn't help thinking it was Jagger's own feelings on his situation seeping from his soul. He bent his head so he could wipe a tear from his eye unseen.

The music changed, Jagger striking a lively tune, one Brick immediately clapped along to. The look in Jagger's eyes, as he rested his gaze upon Brick, said he'd caught how melancholy his first one had rendered Brick, and had switched accordingly. It also made Brick admit to himself that he was falling in love with Jagger.

Which made him all the more determined to win the elf his freedom from the stupid prophecy and its horrible obligations. That wasn't the only thing spurring him on. Brick was beginning to suspect something was happening between them that would account for the odd things he'd noticed, like Jagger acquiring wyvern characteristics, and Brick being able to tolerate the presence of magic. *No. Interspecies bonding is very rare. Almost unheard of.* He tried his best to push the *B* word, and that he'd met Jagger while celebrating the interspecies bonding of two other races, to the back of his mind.

The tunnel widened and broadened into a round cave, and Jagger stopped playing to stare at the long tapering wisps hanging down from the ceiling of the grotto like bunting. He touched one as they passed.

"Rock," he said.

"And these." Brick scraped a finger across a column growing up from the floor and sticking out of the water in a twist. There were several and they looked like teeth, giving the circular cave the look of a mouth. "We'd better get out?"

They didn't have much choice. Steering between the spikes hanging down and the points sticking up would take a lot of effort and skill, and there didn't look anywhere to sail beyond this basin. Jagger got out first, and Brick passed him his bag. He tied the boat up to an iron semi-circle fixed into the wall but wondered if it would float back the way it had come, all on its own.

"I'll be glad to be in the open," Jagger admitted. He stamped a foot. "This feels grassy. It can't be far to the outside."

Walking ahead of him, Brick found it was springy underfoot. He almost tripped over a root and tsked at his clumsiness. He hadn't been that inept around Jagger so far, but maybe his luck was wearing thin. He stumbled again and shook out his foot.

He put it down and tried to bring the other up, only to find a stem around his ankle. Brick twisted his foot to get it out, but it pulled tight, and another shot from the ground and enmeshed his other foot. "This is crazy!" he exclaimed. "Jagger—"

"A little help here?" Jagger called and Brick, not liking the note in his voice, turned…to see him trapped, roots springing from the ground and ensnaring him from his feet to his knees.

Chapter Sixteen

Before Brick could tell Jagger he was coming, and to stay where he was—and then smack himself on his forehead for his stupidity—the stems around his own ankles tightened and lengthened, becoming as thick and long as vines. Maybe they were vines. All Brick knew was that them on him was a horrible, icky feeling, like damp, sharp-smelling snakes not just circling him but slithering up him. It didn't take even half a minute for him to be as immobilized as Jagger was.

"Keep your arms free!" Jagger shouted, vined up to his hips now and struggling to get at his sword. "Do you have a blade?"

Brick didn't, but he had talons. "Apologies in advance!" he shouted to Jagger, just in case he farted or burped in trying to partially shift. But there was no loud parp and no noxious stench, just the ominous rustle of the climbers and shoots slinking from the ground and onto them, and the only smell was the almost musky one of the vegetation. And claws. There were claws. He had claws!

He lunged down and almost overbalanced, saving himself by slapping a hand on a bumpy stone wall at the side of him, scraping his knuckles on its fissures. Fingerlings of tree roots protruded from the wall and grew as he watched, elongating and joining in with the snares coming from the ground to trap him.

"That's not fair—two against one," he railed at the cave. "Well, three—" He'd spotted similar vines swinging down from the roof, snaking in to join the party. He ducked out of the way of one, so it smacked against the wall instead. Brick started struggling in earnest, using both hands to slash through the bonds that were imprisoning him and trying to get him in a full-body lock.

Broad, heavy creepers dropped from above to lash him, the whippings stinging and hurting.

"You okay?" he gasped to Jagger.

"Oh, wonderful," came back to him through gritted teeth. "Just be glad you have short hair…"

The glance Brick could spare showed him that tendrils, stronger than they looked, had shot from the walls and wrapped around locks of Jagger's hair, yanking his head from side to side and back and forth. With those rocking him and other shoots slapping his face, he was having difficulty in using his sword.

Not that it could have been easy under any circumstances to use a sword to cut away tight bindings from his body, without nicking himself on the blade. Unless he'd had lots of practice at it? Brick wrenched his mind from wandering to just what kind of practice Jagger might have had at that, and what kinds of bonds and who'd tied them. He had enough real, urgent problems of his own to deal with at the moment. Like the vine ribboning itself around his face, blocking his nose so he could hardly breathe and binding his eyes to blind him.

Wet trailing down his cheek as he tried to slash through that constraint told him he'd cut his own skin. Worse—a clang then clatter of steel on stone told him Jagger had lost his grip on his sword. "You still okay?" he called.

Silence as the only answer had his heart stopping. Using all his strength, he wrenched his head free of the fronds imprisoning it enough to see Jagger. He was alive, his face wreathed by shoots, preventing him speaking. Another sped around his eyes, cutting off his sight. Then, as if in prearranged synchrony, creepers caught at Jagger's and Brick's arms and pulled them away from their bodies, making any attempt at peeling off their bonds impossible.

Vines as thick as leather belts sprang down from the ceiling in a grim mockery of party decorations. A memory of the bunting and flags decking out the meadow and the palace grounds for the royal nuptials hit Brick and for the first time since he'd started on this stupid adventure, he wondered if he'd ever see his family again.

"Get off me!" Brick shouted against the gag muffling him when the roof creepers caught him and raised him. Them—Jagger was being treated similarly, hoisted high as if he were an acrobat about to spiral down from a vaulted ceiling on a golden ribbon at some fancy dinner. The whip-cracking of hanging tendrils up ahead gave Brick an inkling of what was about to happen. He struggled, but it made absolutely no difference—he was tossed from one set of vines to another and another down the length of the cave.

Some of them seemed to have a sense of humor—they rolled him up, as though he were sausage meat in a cabbage leaf, to be baked in the oven, for the fronds they threw him to then unroll. His head span and he retched, glad his stomach didn't have enough in it to bring up.

Make it stop! he silently implored whatever gods were listening, and whichever were in charge of caves. Or people being held captive by vegetation in caves. *I'll be good, I swear. I'll listen when Father is droning on and on about which kingdoms we should travel to or have visiting us, or when Gules is telling us the national dishes and drinks of those places, or Mother's boasting about her friendships with all the VIPs in each one. I promise!*

Maybe someone heard him, because the last throw tossed them from the large cave and into a smaller one—and more exactly into side-by-side cages hanging from the roof of the cave. The small pens rocked wildly with the momentum of he and Jagger being thrown into them, and gradually swung themselves to a stop. The vegetation whipped itself away from their bodies, slapping and flicking as it did so, and they were alone, in a horrible empty silence.

"Like birds!" His head still spinning and his stomach still roiling, Brick grabbed the bars and tried to bend them. They felt damp and organic in his hands, not inviting to the touch, but he forced himself. He couldn't force the slats though—they didn't budge an inch.

"Forgive me if I don't feel like singing." Jagger got to his knees and cast a look down at the ground below.

It wasn't that far—they could probably jump. Or he could shift. He was a lot stronger in wyvern form too. Strong enough to rip through these stupid cages. Blood spurted from his nose as he tried to change. *Damn.* "I'll keep trying," he promised, holding his forearm over his nose.

"No. Don't. At least not yet." Jagger looked a mess, his curls tangled and wild, his clothes disarrayed. Brick must look worse. "What did that dryad say? I couldn't catch it all?"

"Ash? Oh." Brick understood. "Beware the Lord of All Roots, also known as the Taproot. Ah. We didn't exactly."

"And got caught in his snare. Wasn't there something else?"

"I don't remember," Brick lied. He risked a tiny peep at the other cages in the room. They were all empty…of anything living. Small heaps in some might have once been people but were now bones. *"He'll want to encase you in his snare and keep you down there forever."*

"Ever get the feeling someone or something doesn't want us to reach the Horrorcle?" Jagger asked suddenly.

"What? You think forces are trying to stop our quest?" Brick hardly imagined so. "What's so important about us?"

"Maybe not us, but the foretelling?"

Brick tried to make his brain work on that, to examine it from all angles and see all the consequences, like his parents or Gules or even Milly did with situations. "I don't know," he finally admitted. It sunk in how dire their situation was. He changed position, and it rocked the cage. A few more pushes and he swung near Jagger.

"Catch me?" he asked, and Jagger stuck out a hand and grasped Brick's fingers. "I'm sorry."

Jagger's forehead creased. "For what?"

For so much. Jagger should be out in the world, striding through the palace or carousing in the tavern, larger than life and twice as much fun. Instead, meeting Brick had taken all that away. "If it weren't for me..."

"Hey!" Jagger squeezed his fingers hard. "You're talking like this is it."

Brick...kind of thought it was. He'd met the man he loved, the man he wanted, the man whose life he was predestined to ruin thanks to some stupid old prophecy. And because he'd been running away from that, here they were. There was so much he wanted to tell Jagger. His feelings for him, for one thing. That the bonding process had started—he kind of thought—for another. No, that last would make him mad. No point issuing bad news under the circumstances. He tried to speak but it came out as a slight shrug.

"Look at me."

He made himself obey Jagger.

"If it is, then I'm glad I'm facing it with you," Jagger declared.

"Really? But I'm useless!" Brick blotted a tear from his eye. "I'm clumsy, I get things wrong, I'm too big—"

"Damn right you're big." Jagger's smile was a gleam of starlight in the gloom. "I— What's that?"

"A noise." Brick had no idea how to describe it. He couldn't see anything, but the air felt like it did just before Sylph appeared. It was too much to hope that the Ruby Throne's air elemental servant was popping in to rescue them.

"And noises are never good." Jagger readied himself. "I'm guessing I don't have time now to go into all the things about you I want to mention, so we'll keep that for later, okay?"

"Okay," Brick agreed. Curiosity as to what Jagger would mention gnawed at him. "Erm, good things, right?"

Jagger blew out an exasperated breath. "Yes!"

The air in the cave grew cold and a figure began to manifest.

"The Lord of All Roots, I presume?" Jagger asked.

"Also known as the Taproot," Brick added.

The figure should have looked comical, like someone decked out for a Maying, but the shaggy green man exuded an air of menace. His face was almost flat, not really distinguishable from the leaves of the fronds or roots making it, and branches sprouted from it. Brick was kneeling, still trying to break apart the bars keeping him a prisoner, when the cages holding him and Jagger vanished, and they fell.

He'd been right in that it wasn't far, but it was a distance enough and the cave floor hard enough to whump the breath from him.

"I am *so* tired of falling from things!" Jagger exclaimed.

"I've fallen from more than you have," Brick protested. "I fell from the window in the tavern, and you didn't."

It seemed Jagger didn't like being contradicted. He got to his feet and glared at Brick. "I fell from your back when you shifted in mid-air."

"We both fell from the sky! That puts us the same!" Brick wanted to stomp his foot like Scarlet did.

The Taproot shook a little, as though their bickering annoyed him.

"We'll call it even?" Jagger suggested, his hand on his sword.

Brick gripped the javelin. The Taproot thickened and the air in the cave thinned. The light dimmed everywhere but the figure, as if he were absorbing it. Brick coughed, his throat dry. No—closing. Well, something was making it hard to breathe. He clawed at his throat as though that would help. Next to him, Jagger was on his knees, pulling and snatching at his neck as if trying to loosen invisible bindings choking him.

"Oxygen?" Brisk gasped. "Isit tak' our oxygen?"

"Don't want to find out," Jagger wheezed.

Living things needed air, and that included plants and…flowers. Brick remembered the small pointy ones he'd felt impelled to pick. Struggling, he got them free of his pocket. He hadn't looked at them since he'd taken them and even in this dim greenish light, they glowed the bright pixie-pink he'd imagined they would. Their stems had interlaced, making them into a posy.

He should make a speech, he knew, when making an offering, but that had never been his forte, and he doubted he could now, what with the lack of air in his lungs. He flicked the small bouquet toward the Taproot.

"We bring a gift, sir," he managed.

It fell into the leaves of his feet…and did absolutely nothing. Of course.

I'm sorry! he tried to make his imploring eyes tell Jagger, who looked back at him with not the contempt or anger Brick had expected, but fear. Jagger was as afraid as Brick was.

"Ash?" Jagger gasped.

It took Brick to second to figure out Jagger was asking what else Ash had said. "To give him his due," he managed to utter.

"We bring you your due, sir," Jagger repeated.

"Your due!" Brick yelled with the tiny bit of air left in his windpipe. He sank to his knees and grabbed for Jagger.

"And ask for passage through your realms for our quest!" Jagger added.

Nothing happened. "Again," Brick rasped.

"We bring you your due and ask for passage!" they both got out and heaved in a breath after.

Because they could. There was air! In Brick's lungs and in Jagger's too, he bet, and in the cave.

The Taproot moved and scooped up the posy, its pink making him shine greener and his green making it gleam bright pink.

"We bring you your due and ask for passage for our quest!" they both shouted, and again, louder, then once more, making the roof ring with their cries. And as the echoes died, the Lord of All Roots grew transparent, insubstantial and dematerialized.

"Did...we do it?" Jagger whispered.

Chapter Seventeen

Brick peered all around. "I think so?"

Jagger thought so too. He also thought they were alone, in a gloomy cave, the kind of place he would never normally venture to. It had claw marks on the stone walls, broken spider webs hanging from the roof where water also dripped from cracks, forming pools and puddles on the uneven floor—but never had a dingy, stale-smelling place looked so good. He whooped. "We did it!"

Brick caught his exuberance and hollered too, grabbing hold of Jagger so they both jumped up and down together like elflettes cheering on the palace guards at a training game. Their shouts and yodels filled every nook and cranny of the grimy place.

"You worked out we should bring a gift to a ruler," Jagger said.

Brick scoffed. He should have known that as second nature. It was the sort of protocol that had been drummed into him since hatchhood. Entering another sovereign's territory without so much as a by-your-leave? What could he and Jagger have expected?

"Ash told us. We applied what we learned and used it and believed in what we were doing. Is that all it takes?" Jagger wondered.

"I guess." Brick calmed a little. "My mother's always telling to believe in myself too when situations look daunting."

"You face this kind of stuff at the Ruby Throne?" Jagger asked, incredulous.

"No. More like that I won't fart in front of Ruler Targanent or belch all over Empress Amanyda or break the ceremonial low stools used at the gryphon court by sitting on them when they're *clearly* for resting one's tail spike on. Stuff like that." Brick grinned.

"I see." Jagger gave a slow nod. Brick had mentioned before his difficulties in leading the sort of life expected of him, the kind his family wanted him to, but at least they weren't unkind to him over it. The opposite, in fact. Jagger wasn't exactly sure why this pleased him so much, but he suspected he knew the reason. Brick's happiness and comfort were important to him. *Brick* was important to him. He was falling for the strapping, burly wyvern shifter. No, that wasn't true. He had fallen for him, literally and emotionally.

Adrenaline coursed through him, both at that knowledge and at their escape from that crazy root creature, needing an outlet. He pulled his handsome wyvern shifter to him for a frenzied kiss, all lips and teeth and tongue and *alive*. He couldn't remember his balls aching and his cock filling this much, this fast, ever. He groped Brick's gorgeous rump, cupping and squeezing the cheeks he loved getting his hands on. Being this close pressed him into Brick's chest, and he remembered somewhere else he liked to play, another thing he like toying with.

He pushed Brick's jacket from his shoulders and opened his shirt. *There.* That tiny gleam bisecting Brick's flat nipple, glinting in his chest hair, the golden ring that made Jagger feel like a pirate going after treasure. Brick's indrawn breath, his gasp made Jagger want to see what more sounds he could wring from him. A whole orchestra, he bet.

He bent his head to Brick's warm flesh, using his teeth to slide the hoop through the hole in Brick's nipple, rubbing his chin into the wyvern as he did so. Brick had said he liked Jagger's facial hair and Jagger thought he'd let him experience it all over, on those parts of his body he hadn't yet. Brick was enjoying it here—he was starting to rut on Jagger.

"Damn!" Jagger pulled away. "This isn't really the best place for this, is it?"

"Sure…" Brick went to undo his breeches and Jagger stayed his hand.

"I mean we should get out of here. Get aboveground."

"Oh. Yeah. Yeah." Brick dipped his head.

"Hey. None of that." At Jagger's stern tone, Brick raised his head again. "As soon as we're outside again…" He grinned, more so at Brick's muttered, "*Promise?*" as he began searching for an exit.

"Hey, what about this?" he called, beckoning Jagger over to peer up the narrow chimney-like tunnel. "You'll be okay?"

Jagger nodded. He'd have to be.

"Tell you what, I'll go first, and you can follow my cute ass. How about that?" Brick started to climb.

It seemed to work as a distraction, or maybe Jagger had become used to enclosed spaces, since they'd started this. He definitely felt easier about being in the chimney, and the climb was easy, with the rungs studded into the side and the daylight pulling him on.

He was glad, though, to heave himself out, over the side…where he stared all around at the cave they emerged in. It was small—they could barely stand up in it—and had an entrance on one side. Water dripped from its roof and ran down most of its walls. But it wasn't so much the cave in itself that had him staring…

"Are those little shoes? Like babies' shoes? And children's toys?" Brick nodded at the items.

Jagger took in the objects, on niches, in nooks, and hanging on lines like grotesque gray-white decorations. Water ran down everything. The things looked real, or as if they had been, at one time, before— "How come everything's turned to stone?"

"Because this is a warlock's cave?" Brick whispered, drawing close to him.

"I'm not so sure…" Jagger replied.

"Oh, thank the gods."

"…that it's a cave." Jagger examined the chimney they'd arrived via. It had a pulley fixed to its top, and a stone bucket lay on the ground. "It's an enclosed well."

"*A warlock's well*!" Brick whimpered.

Jagger was more curious about the constant drip of water. He examined a small skipping rope near him. It really was stone.

"Don't touch anything!" Brick yelped. "And don't let any water get on you—that's how it's done! Whatever it touches, it turns to stone."

Jagger scoffed and scooped up a palmful of water from a dip in a rock.

"*No!*" Brick screeched, but too late. Jagger had flung it over him.

"Arrgghh!" Brick screamed, slamming his eyes closed. When nothing happened, he opened them. "Oh. And don't do that!"

"Sorry." But Jagger thought Brick was right—the water was 'doing it' somehow.

"What is this place?" Brick turned in a slow circle. "You live around here. You must know."

"Firstly, I have no idea where we are. Secondly, if we are still in the Forbidden Forest"—Jagger sped up to stop Brick interrupting—"the name should tell you I don't come here! No one from the town does. But yeah, I remember hearing tales when I was an elfling of a well that turned things to stone."

"A warlock's well," Brick repeated.

"Stop saying that! It's— Oh."

"What?" Brick caught his sleeve.

"Just something I heard, some silly gossip, a rumor, in the Cock and Balls."

"Huh?"

"The tavern. A while back. There was talk of a new warlock seen in the forest." He scoffed.

"Erm, yes, that would be me?" came a voice from the entrance hole…belonging to the figure who was straightening up from the crouch he was in to get through the gap.

Jagger bit back his scream more successfully than Brick.

"Ooh, please don't." The man screwed up his face and covered his ears. He took a step toward them.

"Stay where you are, warlock!" ordered Brick.

"I'm Kevin." The man pointed at his chest.

"Stay where you are, Kevin the warlock!" Brick demanded.

"I'm not a warlock. I'm a human."

"Stay where you are, Kevin the…human…?" Brick trailed off.

"You're a *human*?" Jagger had met one when he was much younger but could hardly recall.

"Erm, well, yes, as it were." The human was younger and shorter than both Jagger and Brick and round-shouldered, as if he habitually hunched in on himself. "Sorry to, erm, disappoint, if you were expecting something more along the lines of an *actual* warlock." He grimaced in apology.

"No, that's… Could we talk outside?" Jagger *really* needed to be in the open.

"Oh, of course! Remiss of me. Awful manners," Kevin the human babbled as he exited and waited for them. "Might I ask well, of course I can ask—I mean, would you tell me your names? Not if it's considered rude or taboo, or not done, obviously. I wouldn't want to—"

"Jagger, Brick." Jagger tried to short-cut things. He breathed in the fresh air.

"Brick, Jagger." Brick was trying to help.

"Kevin. Well, you know that." The man smiled, showing uneven teeth.

"How—?"

"I fell through the veil," Kevin answered Jagger's question, before he'd asked it. He patted a fallen log for them to sit on and took a stump opposite.

"*What?*" Jagger was amazed.

"I've heard of that happening," Brick said.

But it was very rare.

"What were you doing?" Jagger asked Kevin.

"When I…" Kevin mimed falling. "Oh, well, not to put too fine a point on it, I was out rambling."

Yeah, Jagger could believe that.

"Rambling is walking." Kevin glanced at him.

Ogres' foreskins, he reads minds! Jagger tried to warn Brick.

"I hear thoughts," Kevin corrected.

"Go on?" Jagger said, trying not to think.

"Well, as it happens, I was cataloging moss." Kevin flashed them both an apologetic wince.

"Moss?" Brick scratched at a tree trunk. "Like this?"

"Well, not exactly like that, because I've never seen that type on my side of the veil, and believe me, I've put in some moss hours." Kevin heaved a sigh. "But to introduce myself properly, and not wishing to blow my own trumpet, I'm Dr. Kevin Wilkinson, curator of bryology at the Bradshaw Herbaria at Dillon University."

He looked from Jagger to Brick at the silence this was met with and Brick and Jagger looked at each other, both of them giving tiny head shakes to the other. No, this human wasn't famous in either of their kingdoms. *Awkward.*

"Now, before you ask or want to ask but don't feel you can, I know, yes, that mosses are different to hornworts and liverworts but bryophytes covers all three. Not lichens. Lichenology is a different field." He glared at them as though they'd contradicted him. This was obviously a sore point.

"Different from…?" Jagger tried.

"The scientific study of, that is, observing, recording, classifying and researching, bryophytes. That's what we bryologists do. In sum. In essence. In a nutshell."

"In a nutshell?" Brick looked confused.

"Never mind the nutshell," Jagger muttered to him. "Kevin..." Saying the name felt odd in his mouth. "But what specifically were you doing when you came through?"

"Oh!" Kevin chuckled. "Funny story, actually. I'm chair of a local bryophyte association, in addition to my work, as a side-line. Just a little hobby, like my moss paintings, which fetch not insubstantial sums for the local fetes and causes. Yes, the association keeps me out of mischief, one might say! And one of the newer members thought she'd seen glittering bristle moss. In *the Midlands*! The Midlands, I ask you." He shook his head. "As if. In the north, *maybe*, at a stretch, but... Oh, those bryo-newbies. Although Katie is more of a bryo-babe... Anyway, so it meant that of course I had to go a-hunting."

"And was it? Was it glittering bristle?" Brick was literally on the edge of his seat. Jagger hadn't realized he liked stories. His heart swelled at the cuteness.

"Was it heck as like!" Kevin clapped his hands together in triumph then looked ashamed. "Oh, pardon my French. Good thing there are no ladies about. Bryology *can* get a little heated."

"Well, what was it?" Brick demanded.

"Silky merkin!" Kevin half-shouted. "You can see why the confusion, of course." He looked from one to the other. "Ah. Well, maybe not."

It was evident Brick couldn't. He sank back.

"And...?" Jagger asked, patting Brick's knee.

"Long story short, I tripped and fell and ended up here, where I can hear thoughts. I got overwhelmed and came to live here as a hermit."

Here where the rumors of a warlock keep people away. Jagger got it. He looked back at the well. "How—?"

"Is everything petrified—turned to stone? The minerals in the water. Lime and magnesium and other stuff. I'm no geologist." Kevin shrugged. "But from what I remember learning at school, the water evaporates on exposure to the air and leaves the lime, and that coats everything it trickles over! It turns it to limestone."

"Huh." Brick looked almost disappointed. "Well, we're sorry to intrude, Kevin the— Kevin."

"Not at all. What, or rather where, if one might make so bold…? Why the…?" Kevin pointed to the well.

Jagger considered. The way things had been going for them, and his suspicion that something was working against them, should he reveal their plans to this stranger? This man…who read, or rather, listened to, thoughts and was being polite about it. *Yeah.* Jagger felt foolish. "We're going to the Cave of the Worlds, to seek the Horrorcle," he said.

"Can you help us?" Brick asked.

Jagger wanted to slap him. With his background, and after what they'd been through so far, Brick should know people did favors *for* favors.

"Oof. Goodness. Crikey." Kevin frowned. "That's rather a way away. Mountains, and all that. Tell you what I can do for you…"

"Yes?" Brick asked.

"Make you a cup of tea." Kevin's happy smile showed all his teeth.

Chapter Eighteen

"Tea?" Brick repeated. "Is it...*moss* tea, by any chance?"

"Indeed it is!" Kevin slapped his hands on his knees and stood. "I can offer it to you upright and erect or prostrate and spreading." He laughed, clutching at a branch to steady himself. "Bryology humor, with their being two classifications of moss. Acrocarps, which grow upright, and Pleurocarpous which grow in a prostrated position." He wiped his eyes and shook his head.

"I'm a bit lonely," he said, abruptly, and clapped his hand over his mouth, his eyes horrified at what he'd blurted out.

"We'd like tea, wouldn't we, Jagger?" Brisk said. He understood lonely.

"Oh, excellent!" Kevin was all smiles again. "I can even rustle us up some biscuits! And yes, they are moss biscuits."

Brick hadn't asked the question, had only been thinking it. *Thought-hearer. Right. Must remember that.*

He followed Kevin, who was rambling on about swan's-neck versus goose-neck, and the naming system he'd invented for the new species of moss he came across. He'd show them his collection…

"This is me. Home sweet…cave." Kevin gestured at the entrance to what looked like a good-sized hollow in a rock face. "Let me show you around. Living area here, sleeping area there, storage area here and there. Compact and bijou, as an estate agent would say! I've been working on laying out the patio, just outside, recently. Well, you know we British and our gardens. Well, perhaps you don't. Sorry. That was presumptuous of me. Have you ever met, well—there are no two ways to say it—a human?"

"Oh yes!" Brick remembered an occasion. He'd been a fledgling at the time. They'd had visitors who'd brought one with them. "I think the one I met must have been a baby. We can work it out—how old are you when you grow the long arms?" He held his up to compare it with Kevin's. "Yours are full-grown now, right?"

"Erm…" Kevin looked at Jagger, who shook his head in bemusement.

"And you walk normally. You don't hop," Brick continued.

"I…don't…*hop*?"

"Oh, I did see an adult, too!" Brick remembered more now. "A female adult. She carried her son in a pouch, right here." He patted his stomach. "They were brown-skinned, and a bit hairier than you. And they had tails."

"Ah." Kevin bit his bottom lip. "That's not… What you saw was a kangaroo. An animal."

"Not a human?" Brick held up his hands like paws and jumped on both feet.

"Not a human." Kevin gathered what he needed and led them outside again.

"I think you upset him," Jagger muttered. "How would you like it if someone thought you started off as a lizard, before you became wyvern?"

"Or when people think elves are the same as pixies and fairies." Brick understood his *faux pas*. His latest in a long line. He closed his eyes in shame. This was why he'd be a disaster to any mate, anywhere, so to think of him at the elven palace…

"No offense taken. In truth, we're just like you." Kevin looked up from where he was pouring hot water from the pan boiling on the fire into a pot warming on a stone at the side. "Well, not like you two exactly. Much feebler. And not so flamboyant."

In staring at them, he seemed to forget he was still holding a hot pan and jerked, as if burned. "No problem, not with the abundance of Sphagnum about," he declared, grabbing up a handful of dark green stuff and curling his palm over it. "Nature's antiseptic. You know, I always thought that as long as I had my moss, I'd be happy, and I am, but it's nice to have company."

He shushed them with a finger to his lips as he counted down the time to let their moss tea infuse and pour it. "No clocks in the forest, as the Bard of Avon observed. And yes, all the stereotypes about Brits and their cuppas are true!"

"I always thought moss would taste like dirty water," Brick commented, taking a sip…and almost gagging.

"Oh, it does yeah." Kevin winced as he drank. "Very dirty water like sweaty underwear has been soaked in it, and then slugs frolicked in it, I've come to think." He drained his cup. "More?"

They both declined a second cup.

"You're staying for lunch, of course?" Kevin asked.

Finally the human was speaking his language. Brick accepted the invitation happily. "Oh…it's not moss, is it?" he asked, crossing his fingers.

"No." Kevin huffed as if offended. "Rabbit. Flavored with herbs."

"Not with herby moss?" Brick checked, and Kevin laughed. A lot.

He laughed some more, crying fat tears at the joke, and finally wiped his face. "Come on. Lunch is roasting in the fire, so let's go to the bar for a quick one while it cooks."

"Don't go imagining a tavern or pub. I wouldn't want you to get disappointed," Jagger murmured to Brick.

Brick was glad he had when Kevin showed them a tall plant with thick, curled-over leaves he slashed with a sharp stone to squeeze the sweet juice from. He squirted this into his mouth, to drink.

"Meet Belinda." Kevin introduced them to the faucet. "Named after a co-worker of mine who was always ready for a drink!"

"I don't think he means in exactly this way," Jagger told Brick, who was trying not to imagine Kevin sneaking up on a human woman with his hand-ax.

Kevin had tied bits of wood together with long, thin frond-leaves to make chairs and set them around the plant. "Now, if only I could get the daily paper, this would be perfect." He sighed.

* * * *

Brick thought the meal Kevin served, with them all sitting cross-legged around the fire a little later was perfect. Roast kannin and brambor, or rabbit and potatoes, as the human called it, and, as Kevin had cooked two kannin, a whole rabbit just for him. He moaned in joy as he held it in both hands, ripping the meat from the bones with his teeth. He moaned louder when he chewed.

"That's the rosemary and sage," Kevin said, beaming proudly.

Brick burped.

"And…that's the garlic." Kevin grimaced.

"Sorry," Jagger said, on behalf of Brick, whose mouth was full.

"Oh no." Kevin waved Jagger's apology away with his knife. "It's nice to see a hearty appetite. I imagine it takes a lot to fill him, keep him satisfied."

"I do my best." Jagger winked.

Brick half-twisted and half-jumped at that and dropped his kannin in the fire. With a howl of loss, he leaped up to get it, beating out the flames to snatch it back. "Oh, sorry," he said, realizing he'd extinguished most of the fire. *Typical Brick.* His face heated at his clumsiness.

"You know, I wasn't meaning… I wouldn't ask… Oh, gracious." Kevin subsided into a heap of half-uttered twittering.

"I'd like to explore," Jagger said.

"…the…surroundings, you mean?" Kevin said, eventually, waving a hand in the air to indicate the forest. "Not, well, anything else?" He dropped his gaze.

Brick choked, trying to speak with his mouth full and this time spat meat into what was left of the fire.

"Be my guest. Oh wait—you are!" Kevin grinned again, this time showing not only all his teeth, but the bits of meat trapped in two of them.

* * * *

"And guests shouldn't do chores," Kevin protested later to Brick, who insisted on helping clear away.

"And royal-adjacent elves shouldn't stick Ruby Throne wyvern shifters with clean-up," Brick muttered. Jagger had gone to take a look around. Brick tipped the remnants onto the midden, the domestic waste pile Kevin had shaped in a heap.

"Jagger, you're talking about? The…man, sorry, elf, you're in love with, yes?" Kevin sat back on his heels where he was patting firm the sides of his dump. "Oh, you…you did know? That you, well, as the poets might put it—"

"Yeah." Brick didn't think he could stomach poetry. It might taste like moss tea. "I guess so." He sighed.

"Oh." Kevin tilted his head to regard him. "Aren't wyvern shifters happy when they're in love, and by the side of the person they love?"

"Well, that's kind of the thing." Brick sat. "He's only by my side because he has to be. It's a long story but there's a foretelling that my people and his make an alliance through us."

"A marriage of state. Oh." Kevin thought for a bit. "You know, it was through a marriage treaty that Britain got tea. So these arrangements aren't all bad. I mean, obviously they shore up alliances between two nations or kingdoms or whatever as well. And bring territory, for instance. It's not just about tea. Sorry to bring that into it." He winced.

"*Make* an alliance?" Kevin asked, a minute later. "You haven't made it yet? Well, I mean, I can tell you've 'made it', as the kids say. Or used to say. They no doubt have different slang now. Or the same words, but they don't mean the same. Like when 'sick' used to mean bad and now it means good."

"We're trying to stop it. The agreement. Trying to challenge the prophecy. Yes, I'm in love with him. But him, and me? Him forced to endure me for ever more? I couldn't force him to do that. I couldn't trap him," burst from Brick.

He had more he wanted to say, and it was nice to have someone to talk to, but he glimpsed Jagger returning and shut up. He widened his eyes and jerked his head at Kevin, trying to convey the message that Jagger was nearby, then felt stupid. How many more times did he need to remind himself that Kevin was a thought reader!

"*Listener.* I don't *read—*" Kevin shut up. He stood. "I'm fascinated to meet a wyvern shifter! Can you tell me something about wyverns? I'm keeping a journal and there's not really a great deal to write about. Apart from my moss hunting, I mean. But I get the feeling wyverns are mystical?"

"That's a polite way of putting it." Jagger joined them and helped Brick to his feet. "There's a lot of supernatural stuff associated with any shifter and especially the noble ones, the flying beasts. Yeah, there's a thing to do with bonding, right? With mating?"

Is there a reason he's asking that? Brick's heart stuttered, then sped at the thought that Jagger might be beginning to suspect the same thing Brick did. No, what Brick thought he *knew*—that the soul-bond had started. *Soul blend,* Brick had always thought of it, the way wyverns took on some characteristics of their mate.

Cerise, for instance had acquired enough of Carnell's color to become a beautiful red, unknown in the kingdom for a century, and Carnell had imbibed Cerise's strategic way of thinking and prowess with statecraft. Brick's grandfather, Garnet, had lost most of his tail in the Territory Wars, and yet once he'd bonded with Coral—originally Claryssa—it had grown back, looking like her slimmer one.

Jagger was an elf, yet Brick had seen him assume wyvern form, and possess a wyvern shadow, just as Brick's had looked elven. They'd also been able to see into each other's minds, at times. It all added up. *To trouble. To heartbreak. To guilt.*

"Brick?" Jagger was looking puzzled and a little concerned.

"Breath." Brick nodded, too fast and too much. "There's a thing called wyvern breath we manifest when we're bonded. It can do, well, *something*. My father has storm breath. Not like a dragon," he clarified, anticipating their questions. "It's not fire. It's a strong, cold wind, like a hurricane, and sweeps away all in its path. Enemies, weapons…" He shrugged.

Flad had said that with Brick's luck, he'd get morning breath, but that would be good—he could annihilate his foes with a blast of that. The memory made him smile. A little.

"That's amazing." Kevin had a small homemade-looking notebook in his hand and was scribbling notes on the dried leaves with a red feather he kept dipping into a container of dark-blue dye. It smelled like kholnfish and was probably extracted from its liver. "Oh, I hope you don't mind…? Only this is so exciting!"

He looked up after a minute. "Do elves have any mating, erm, bonding things, like that?"

"There is!" It was Brick who spoke, not Jagger. "I think. Something about tears, right? I was trying to remember earlier."

"No. Maybe some past superstition." Jagger turned. "That water reservoir back that way, it's fine to use, right?"

"Uh-huh." Kevin nodded. "I do. It's nice and deep."

"Brick, would you like to come there with me?" His grin was dirty, and Brick had no trouble understanding what kind of 'coming' Jagger wanted to do there.

"'Companions with benefits.'" Kevin was scribbling the phrase down.

Brick tried not to feel sad at where Kevin must have 'heard' that. "Yes, please," he answered Jagger.

Despite his longing, his knowledge that the two of them could never be more than temporary companions and his guilt, he'd 'come' anywhere with Jagger.

Chapter Nineteen

"Haven't we had enough of water?" Brick asked as they walked. "The Welling River—and its weir—and that underground stream?"

"This is different. Pretty." Jagger gave up on explaining, Brick would see it soon enough. Sooner—"Race you! And no wyvern ways—"

"And no elven magic!" Brick was already running.

He was quick, considering he was so burly, and Jagger thought Brick might just have beaten him to the edge of the grassy bank, where he stopped and cocked his head, listening to what was down below.

"It's a *waterfall*?" he asked, turning to Jagger.

"Yes, but nothing like the weir. And I checked it out just now." Should he explain to Brick that he'd accessed his elven magic—the best he could, being far from an expert user—to try to sense any threats or other magic in the surroundings? "It's fine," he compromised by saying. "And probably not like you're imagining, sheets of water roaring down a sharp rockface from shelf to shelf. Go on, take a look."

Brick peered and his jaw dropped as Jagger's had earlier on seeing the round lake, its turquoise water calm and glinting with sunlight and scattered here and there with yellow flowers from the slim trees around the edges that were nodding their branches to it. Darting gleams suggested fish dancing under the surface of the water.

But Brick was pointing at the far end, where a half-dozen streams of water sprayed out from among the leafy fronds of one steep side, cascading down the verdant wall like a row of showers. Sunlight made the stray drops into diamonds and where the streams hit the water of the lake, there was no angry churning or frothing, but instead soft splashes and thick ripples.

"I see. And is the race still on?"

Jagger didn't need to ask what Brick meant—the wyvern was already half-undressed. He shed more of his clothes as he darted away from the grassy edge, and the remainder as he ran back to it, so by the time he launched himself into the air, he was naked. As was Jagger, their two bodies twisting in their descent so they both dived into the water head-first.

The water was colder than its inviting appearance had made it look, but the impact was far from unpleasant. Jagger surfaced first, whooping in delight and shaking his hair back from his face. Brick's head popped up seconds later, along with an arm, the hand of which he clamped to the top of Jagger's head and pushed him under.

Jagger emerged spluttering. "Why you…"

But Brick was off, swimming with strong pulls of his arms through the water, leaving Jagger in his wake, to catch him if he could. Jagger preferred to watch, but then there was nothing to see when Brick duck-dived under.

"I thought wyverns had affinity with the air, not this element!" Jagger called, using his arms to keep afloat and peering all around for Brick. He saw a flicker under the surface and twirled around, but not fast enough. With a roar, Brick soared free of the water and on top of him, dragging him down.

They rolled and twisted, playing underwater and above-water tag. Jagger got in a sly hit and dived away, only to be caught by an ankle and pulled back, then held hard against Brick's body. He slithered around to face him, curious how the press of Brick's nipple piercing would feel against his damp skin. He didn't get a chance to experience it before Brick slipped under the surface again, and Jagger yelled out in surprise as a hand cupped his balls.

Brick's hand. Just as it was Brick's mouth sucking the tip of Jagger's erect cock in, licking the crown then taking the length deep. Him doing this in a pool was a totally different blow job. Brick's mouth on his shaft felt both hotter and cooler than usual—hotter in comparison to the water all around them, keeping them afloat, and cooler because them being in this pool lowered both their temperatures, including the heat of Brick's mouth.

"Brick..." Jagger said the wyvern's name like a prayer when Brick deep-throated him. He forgot to tread water when Brick rubbed a finger over his hole and would have sunk if Brick hadn't been clamped to him. He peered at Brick's watery, barely discernible shape just as bubbles floated up and popped in a short string. So wyverns didn't have gills.

Brick pressed in the finger he was rubbing around Jagger's hole, just a sly tickle inside Jagger's channel, then forging deeper. Again, being in water gave this a different feeling, and doing it without lube made it…not hurt, because Brick was being careful, but made Jagger want more. He wanted Brick's cock inside him hard and strong, taking him, making him Brick's.

And that thought had him rocking them both when he tried to fuck Brick's throat and himself, on Brick's finger. Jagger's motions turned jerky, his release summoned from him. Gods, his orgasm was going to be epic—until Brick stopped that tight suction on his dick. He broke the surface of the water, with a massive heave of gasped-in breath.

Jagger's mouth dropped open at the sight. Brick looked like some god, existing in all the elements at once, water streaming from him, his lips swollen. The hand he'd cradled Jagger's nuts with was now a tight band around the base of his cock, stopping him coming…and he was still penetrating Jagger's ass.

Stymied, stimulated, Jagger almost broke. He stared into Brick's beautiful yellow-gold eyes, reading his own desires and needs there, until Brick closed them, took in another breath and submerged himself again.

The torture started again too, Brick sucking him deep and penetrating him farther, enough to rub over the bump inside his channel that had him keening his pleasure-pain to the hills. But Brick showed no mercy, tearing his mouth free and bobbing up from under the water to tread water alongside Jagger just as Jagger's climax started. Only this time, when Jagger was ready to weep with frustration, Brick, still locking gazes with him, inserted another finger inside him, their thickness stretching him.

"Brick..." Jagger wasn't too proud to beg. He writhed, as much as he could in the water's embrace, his cock trembling, and when Brick bent his head again, Jagger almost screamed. Then, when Brick relaxed his fingers from the constricting circle they'd made around the base of Jagger's shaft, the band that had held his climax at bay, and worked his cock like he owned it, Jagger did scream.

He thrust, his body jerking with the force of the orgasm that ripped through him. His ass clamped on Brick's fingers lodged in him, and cum pulsed from the head of his dick. It shot onto Brick's face, which Brick was bending low to receive it. He caught some in his open mouth, on his ready tongue, but took the bulk of it on his face, even the last pulses he wrung from it. And all the time, he kept his eyes turned up to Jagger's, even when he slid his fingers free of his channel.

Brick dripping with his release was the most erotic sight Jagger had ever seen. No, he had to scratch that thought a second later when Brick flicked out his tongue to lick at the cum slipped down. And his tongue... Jagger blinked at its length and suggestion of a split in its tip. He'd thought before that Brick had... Whatever this was, he couldn't believe it but fucking *loved* it. His entire body was trembling, and his balls *hurt* with how hard he'd come, but he loved that too.

"You okay?" Brick asked, scooping water to splash on his face and wash Jagger's release from it.

"Yes." *Just about.*

"Good. Because you know what?" The pool splashed and rippled about them as Brick rubbed against him. Gods, he was huge. It seemed bringing Jagger to a realms-shattering orgasm and tasting his cum had enflamed him.

"You're horny?" Jagger guessed.

"Yeah." Brick rubbed a little more. "How about you?"

Jagger pressed back. His cock was trying its best to fill. "I could fuck, yeah."

He was still catching his breath, and his heart was still slowing to its normal rate when they began swimming toward the far wall, where the water arced down. Well, paddling and making rowing strokes with their arms. Jagger was too spent for athletics and supposed Brick too pent-up. *Huh, not for long.* He raised his head to judge how far away they were when he caught sight of their reflections, cast ahead on the sun-dappled water.

Only…they weren't exactly themselves. Both of them, him and Brick, reflected as two winged wyverns. Why was that? No, a better question—how was that possible? And it was a question he thought he might have the answer to, because it was the same reason how he and Brick had been able to commune mind to mind, which they had done a couple of times.

Added up, it could only mean one thing— But then they reached the sandy ground of what passed for a shore, hugging the foot of the far wall's steep hillside, and Brick was on him, pinning him down.

"Ogres' armpits!" he hissed. "Your bag's up there, with our clothes."

And the lube. Yeah, Brick fingering him when Jagger being submerged in water had eased entry was one thing, but a dry fuck was another. "There'll be something here. See the shower area?"

Brick, despite his discomfort, huffed out a laugh. The recessed area behind one of the biggest cascading jets of water wasn't large or deep enough to be a cave, for which Jagger was grateful. He'd had enough of caves. But it did look like a bathroom shower. "The ledges," Brick said, nodding in understanding. "Don't go anywhere…"

Jagger wouldn't and couldn't. He watched Brick walk behind the curtain of water, admiring how the spray broke over his huge hard on, and search the 'shelves'.

"Towel, soap *and* lube!" he called through the streaming water. "Guessing Kevin 'comes' here a lot…"

He was back with Jagger in a second and raised an eyebrow to see him patting the ground in front of a large rock, the gesture inviting.

"What? I fancy a ride," Jagger said.

"Won't be a long one," Brick warned him, sitting and using the rock as a back support.

"I wouldn't say that. It's plenty long and thick enough for me." Jagger took up the small pot, wondering briefly which fruit it had once been the kernel of, and scooped out some of the thick ointment.

Brick moaned when Jagger spread it over his cock. "Don't…tease…" he hissed, pulsing in Jagger's fist.

"I'm not," Jagger replied, running his slicked fingers over his ass cheek, round to his hole. "If I were teasing, I'd turn around, like this…"

Brick's whimper told Jagger he was watching him prep himself. It made Jagger put on a show, easing two then three fingers in. He hurried—Brick's cock would feel better. *Did* feel better, and thicker and bigger as he straddled Brick and sank down, taking the fat tip of his cock in his hole. He bore down, and Brick bucked up, so Jagger could take the head then the shaft in his passage.

"What...you're..." Brick's sentence finished in a groan.

"Clenching," Jagger said, gritting his teeth too. His breath rushed from him when he took all of Brick in. He clamped harder, making his walls work Brick. He raised up, his thighs flexing, then slammed down, Brick's thick cock stuffing him to the brim and spreading him wide open.

He rode Brick hard and knew it wouldn't last long. But it couldn't, not with the ecstasy building, starting in his balls and— No. Not *his* balls. They were filling sure, but he was experiencing *Brick's* feelings, living his pleasure, as his dick throbbed, and he lit up from the inside out.

Brick grabbed Jagger's hips to thrust up into him harder, once, twice, then he yelled, throwing his head back, the tendons in his neck standing out. He arched and came inside Jagger, his cum jetting from him, heating Jagger. Brick shuddered to stillness before easing Jagger off him to one side.

He collapsed next to him, both of them face to face and Brick was still panting when he closed the gap between them and licked the tip of Jagger's nose.

"Hey!" Jagger swiped at it. "That a wyvern thing?"

"I dunno." Brick sent him a tired smile. "Think I went to kiss it and instinct took over?"

Jagger turned onto his back, and Brick copied him, their hands touching. Jagger needed the space, slight as it was to think things over. Things like the mate-bond, which he was almost sure was forming. *No. It can't be.* Could it?

Because that would be against everything he wanted. Wouldn't it? Jagger tried to squash down the thoughts that bonding his life with Brick's would be far from the death-by-boredom sentence he'd always seen the mate-tie as, but they rose to the surface, like bubbles in the water.

There was one important piece of elf lore that would be the final proof, if it happened. So until it did—which it probably wouldn't—there was no need to do anything. To say anything. Which was good because Jagger, for all his dash and swagger…was feeling afraid.

Chapter Twenty

"Ohhhh yessss!" Brick's half-groan, half-sigh of satisfaction filled the small cave to its ceiling. "A proper bed again!" The long, thick, woven-frond-covered moss tuffet—what else?—in Kevin's cave was nothing compared to Brick's bed back home. Hells, it didn't even compare to the chipped wooden frame with its well-used mattress at the Cock and Balls. But after all he and Jagger had endured so far on their quest, and the lack of respite they were getting while enduring it, this was like the finest silk stuffed with the softest swans' down.

He wriggled deeper into the heap, admiring both the ingenuity of the bed and its flax covers that Kevin had made. Jagger was a little quiet, Brick thought. He had been since they'd left the pool, with its very steep bank that had been so easy to jump down but so tiring to climb back up.

"Once again, my apologies for failing to mention the steps cut into the northern wall, that make climbing up a breeze," Kevin apologized, his contrite voice coming from where he was bedding down in the living area, nearer to the cave's entrance. "And no, you're not putting me out. I'm happy for the both of you to take my bed."

How happy...and why? Brick couldn't help thinking, even though he knew Kevin could 'hear' his thoughts. Brick wasn't as free and easy as a lot of wyverns were, including his family. No—his sisters. Gules was a little more...correct, was the polite way of putting it. And Brick shared Scarlet's mindset that he really didn't want to know what his parents got up to sex-wise. So if Kevin the human had any ideas about watching them, or—gods above and below—getting involved, Brick wasn't...up for it.

He wasn't a prude. He'd had a couple of threesomes, including one where the third had been a girl...and he didn't understand what his sister Milly saw in it. She was always part of a throuple, usually with another girl and a guy, although her last relationship had been with Albin and Casimir, both of whom she'd towered over and bossed around.

Flad had said, "*When Milly says jump, they do. Her,*" and "*Milly isn't so much the wyvern meat in the sandwich as she is the whole sandwich, and Albin and Casimir the dressing and condiments.*" She had been in a good mood for those few months, Brick recalled. Having her every whim catered to and every fleeting curiosity satisfied would do that.

Olahf had been into exhibitionism...well, probably more into the kind of gatherings where people could see him fuck the youngest son of the Ruby Throne. Brick had been fine with the voyeurism, with others watching. It had spurred him on, he thought, and had the added bonus of making Flad envious. He didn't get invites to *those* kinds of parties.

But Brick wouldn't be too happy with anyone seeing or hearing him have sex with Jagger tonight. It wasn't a performance. It was wild and spontaneous and wholly them. For as long as the quest lasted. *No. No looking ahead, anticipating bad things.* He turned to Jagger, at his side.

"All right?" he asked in a low voice.

"Umm." Jagger was lying on his back, his arms folded behind his head. He jerked his chin upward. "This is relaxing."

Brick followed Jagger's gaze and agreed. Kevin had hammered luminescent gemstones into the cave ceiling, a mix of different shades, and the pale and swirls and spirals he'd created, glowing softly with an occasional gleam of amber or glint of dull emerald, drew the eye and held it. Moonbeams came in through the cave mouth, bathing the front in a milky light and filtering through to where he and Jagger lay.

He had a nicely full belly. Kevin had baked mahi, the golden fish they'd seen in the pool, and which changed color when caught, and when heated during cooking, and again when cooled. He'd shyly proffered a jar of his homemade beech leaf wine, saying several times and in several different ways that he was no vintner, no winemaker and certainly no oenologist, but he believed it wasn't totally undrinkable so if they'd be so kind as to indulge him…

It had been better than the tea, was the kindest comment Brick could come up with.

And so Brick lay replete and content and now—with a little nudging and elbowing to get Jagger to turn onto his side—the big spoon to Jagger's smaller one and—

Oh. He hoped that thought didn't sound sexual, as if they were rubbing one out on the other. He'd hate to be making Kevin think…*things.*

"Don't mind me," Kevin said, making Brick jump. "I'll be out like a light."

"Oh. Right. That's— Yes…" Brick shrugged, and amusement rippled through Jagger, in Brick's arms.

"You sound like him," he murmured, giving a tiny head toss in Kevin's direction. "And lucky Kevin, getting to sleep so quickly."

Tiny grunts and deep breaths that could easily become gentle snores were already drifting over from the other half of the cave.

"I don't think I can get off like that," Jagger continued, wriggling so he could see Brick's face.

"Oh no?" Arousal flared, making Brick shiver in anticipation.

"No. Not unless I get off…first…" The sparkle in Jagger's eyes rivalled any moon rock or star dust, and Brick's breath caught when Jagger rolled him onto his side and tugged at the shorts Brick had donned for modesty. "You knew what you were doing just then, breathing onto my ear tips," he purred into Brick's ear. "You were all but licking them. Going to take a nip…"

Brick hadn't been. Much. "I wasn't," he protested. "I was trying to settle to sleep."

"Ah, yes." Finished removing his shorts, Jagger sent tremors through Brick when he came back up from his feet…taking tiny bites to mark his way and bigger ones of Brick's ass cheeks. "You're tired after all that exercise earlier. So just lie back and let me do all the work…"

* * * *

"C'n feel y' smilin'," whispered Brick a little later.

Jagger supposed he could, with his face pressed into Brick's skin from where he was stretched out over his back, his cock still in his ass. Brick was half-sleeping.

"Wyvern stamina, my left nut," Jagger huffed.

"Elf insat…insatiab…" Brick was fully asleep.

Jagger wasn't far behind, even though his dick was loath to relinquish its sheath. He'd come twice, gentle, easy orgasms, and his cock had softened, but didn't want to slip free of the warm haven that was Brick's ass.

Falling asleep with a partner was already intimate, but this was closeness like Jagger had never known. And yet it had been like that with Brick right from the first. They'd gone to sleep touching and holding hands. Jagger forced himself to separate from Brick and even then his cock gave a few last pulses as he slid out. He didn't know when he'd fallen asleep or even exactly realize that he had, but he must have, because he woke up, crying, tears slipping from his eyes.

"Whhaassup?" came from the slumbering wyvern at his side.

"Nothing. Go back to sleep," Jagger ordered. As soon as heavy breathing told him Brick was sleeping, Jagger rolled free of the bed, pulled on his breeches and made his way out of the cave. What he needed to do…he didn't want anyone to see. His heart thumped when a figure twitched near the cave's mouth. *Kevin.* He'd almost forgotten about the human, but he managed to sneak past him.

Elves didn't cry. They couldn't. Oh, it wasn't that they were too tough, too macho. They experienced the full range of emotion. Well, some did. He didn't. Or hadn't… Aware he was trying to procrastinate, he checked his racing thoughts and stood still in the glade he'd rushed to, taking a deep breath to center himself.

He'd never manifested tear-globes before…because that was what elves did when they were bonded. It was something that enabled them to help their mate. He got a shaky finger to his cheek and felt the tell-tale crystals there. *Bonded…* It tolled like a bell.

Brick wouldn't want him. Other species wanted an elf, sure, and once they'd had one, they checked it off their list and moved on. What did Jagger have to offer? He was royal-adjacent…and Brick was ruling family. *Also, we wouldn't have bonded without all this,* he thought, angrily.

Shit. This was messed up. His tears were welling up, and he collected them on his fingertips, shaking them into his other hand one by one. Soon his cupped palm was full. He examined them, seeing one was blood-red. What the hells did that mean? He closed his palm and squeezed it tight, crushing the crystals, then shook it.

When he opened it, it held a globe, like a crystal ball, but containing a picture, like the transparent spheres he'd seen once, trinkets that had miniature scenes inside them for people to marvel at. Those were to be shaken, if he recalled rightly, to make snow fall on the houses or scenery. Just like this one. He shook it too.

Only, this didn't feature some cute, pretty scene to be admired. Jagger searched for a glowstone, a triboluminescent rock that would generate light when it was rubbed and got rid of some of the adrenaline coursing through him by rolling it violently against his leg. He set it high on a branch when it shone, and its amber beam was enough to show him what he'd feared.

Him and Brick, fighting, struggling to hold off an army, one that was none the less deadly for being invisible. *More so,* Jagger thought. The struggle was prolonged and vicious, fought with weapons and hand to hand combat and ended…with Brick killed. Jagger stared hard and long into the tearglobe, but the scene replayed over and over. Finally he dropped the sphere and used the glowstone to smash it, crushing it to nothing. Not that that would change anything though.

His mouth dry and his heart heavy, Jagger crept back to the cave and Brick's side, careful not to wake him and determined to do whatever it took to keep him safe.

He lay awake until daybreak.

* * * *

"Everyone ready for breakfast?" called Kevin from just outside.

Jagger tried to work out what time it was. *Early.*

"Well, I mean, are you both ready for breakfast? If you see what I mean." Kevin asked, sounding apologetic again, "*Everybody* implies there's a lot of us, doesn't it?"

Brick stretched and rolled his eyes at Jagger. "He started early." He stopped and sniffed. "I smell food. Like, real food."

"Moss toast? Moss cereal?" Jagger pulled on the rest of his clothes.

"No!" Brick raced out to the patio, skidding to a stop at the platters of food. "Bacon, sausage, eggs? Am I hallucinating?

"And grilled tomatoes. And no." Kevin set the final napkin down. "I treat myself once in a while to a meal from the Spotted Dwarf, in the local town."

"You went there and back already?" Jagger couldn't believe it.

"Oh, goodness no!" Kevin pulled out chairs for them. "I use the wraiths. You know they have a company you can make food orders through?"

"They do?" Brick asked. "Wraiths? Like ghosts?"

"Indeed, yes. They collect your order from ghost kitchens and bring it to you. I call it Deliverboo." Kevin sat. "Oh, just my little joke." When they frowned in puzzlement, he sighed. "Sometimes, I *really* wish there were other humans around."

The meal was delicious—crisp bacon, herby sausages, soft eggs, juicy tomatoes—but Jagger didn't have much appetite. He forced himself to eat, though, and thanked Kevin for the meal and the sandwiches he gave them for the journey.

"You'll need all your strength." Kevin looked into the distance, toward the mountains. He was alone with Jagger, Brick having gone to take the waste to the trash heap. "And you're sure this is what you want to do? Because, and although I know less than nothing about prophecies and forewarning, or whatever it is, I do know that you and Brick—"

"Are companions with benefits, yes." Because if he wasn't Brick's bonded, then he couldn't see his fate, and what he'd seen—no, *thought* he'd seen—wouldn't *be* his fate. *Right?* He looked up at a footstep. Brick had returned. "Ready?" he asked him.

Brick nodded. "The final stretch," he said, his voice as flat as Jagger felt. "Nearly over."

Chapter Twenty-One

Companions with benefits. Jagger had said it. *More than once. He* proposed *it.* So yeah, that was all they were. *Or could be. Or should be.* No one would want to be bonded to Brick. No one deserved to be bonded to him, whether through some mystic wyvern crap or some equally mystic prophecy crap. Brick sneaked looks at Jagger as they trudged through the forest and to the foothills of the Crosswise Mountains. Jagger was silent too. He'd seemed to become quieter the nearer they got to their destination.

Brick and Jagger trudged farther and Brick's thoughts whirled around the foretelling, like carrion birds circling a wounded animal. Did he want the prophecy to be true or false? What would hurt less? He knew Jagger wasn't for him, so while being told *no, that's a wrong interpretation of the prediction*, would be a kick in the teeth, he suspected that learning *yes, you got it right! Here's a cookie and a life partner, you lucky wyvern*, would be more painful and for longer. Keeping Jagger shackled him to him was nothing short of cruelty, for both parties.

His spirits grew heavier as the terrain grew rougher. All the things he'd done wrong, all the mistakes he'd made on their quest so far played in his mind. Only yesterday, Jagger had had to help Kevin re-lay and relight the fire, after Brick had put it out by dropping his food into it then retrieving it. Oh, and before that, he'd belched. He would have closed his eyes in shame, but that would have made the images clearer and sharper.

"Steep." Jagger tipped his head back and shaded his eyes, as if trying to see up the mountain. Clouds capped its peak. "The Cave of the Worlds just has to be somewhere like that, of course. It can't be in the cellar of a tavern or the back room of a beauty salon."

"Yes. I mean no." Brick made an effort to pull himself together. "It's high, yeah."

Jagger shot him a sidelong glance. "Could you…try to shift? It'd be so much easier if we could fly there. Oh, not if it's painful, of course. I—"

"Yes." Brick held up a hand to stop Jagger. He didn't need to hear Jagger apologizing for asking him to do something that should have been a breeze to his kind, something that wasn't even second nature to wyverns, but part of them, for earth's sake. "You might want to stand back."

"Of the wingspan? Or the tail length?" Jagger backed off.

"Something like that," Brick replied, rather than say *blast range. And you probably want to hold your nose.* He tried to assume his first form, focusing on the shift. Nothing happened.

"Neeeeaarggh!" burst from between his clenched teeth as he tried harder…to no avail.

"Look, it's no prob— "

"No!" Brick half-yelled at Jagger, who was trying to brush things off. "I got this!" He wiped away what he thought was a drop of blood from one nostril, to discover it was snot. Great. Just great. He was a majestic wyvern, for gods' sake! One of the noble beasts, as Jagger had said, with scales and talons and pointy teeth and— *"Wiinnnggss!"*

He had them, *and* a tail *and* ridges *and* a large snout! He flapped his wings, and as soon as they met, over his broad head, he lost his wyvern self and shrank back into his other-form. Not a problem, he could try again. He clenched his fists and gritted his teeth, but then Jagger was there, right in his face.

"Stop. Right now." He grabbed Brick's upper arms. "I'm sorry I asked."

"Because I'm such a failure?"

"No, because I don't like you putting yourself under that kind of strain. You've burst blood vessels in your eyes and you look like you're about to shit yourself."

"I feel like it too," Brick muttered, giving a surreptitious shimmy to check his pants. *No, all clear.* Seeing Jagger watching him made him lash out in his shame. "Can't you do something? Some elf magic?"

The laugh Jagger gave was short and didn't sound amused. "Hardly. Look, let's just walk, okay?"

"Fine by me," Brick announced, setting off with a hard stomp…and getting his foot stuck in mud. The squelching, sucking noise it made when he tugged it free was obscene, and the brown liquid splatters sprayed on his pants by him shaking his soiled boot made him look as though he *had* crapped himself.

"Great. Just great. Let's hope there's no dress code at the cave."

The air grew danker and grayer and the going got harder the more they ascended. Vegetation grew scarcer, and the sightings of mountain goats and rabbits less frequent. The route they were following, courtesy of Kevin and the map he'd scratched into the side of a soft rockface for them, became an actual mountain path, and would soon be a pass, tight and narrow, between some of the peaks up ahead. Underfoot was alternately boggy and slippery, the latter due to the deposits of broken rock fragments that littered the way. Some were large and easy to see and step over, while the smaller bits—

"Brick!" Jagger made a dart for him as he skidded on scree.

He didn't manage to stop him, and Brick's momentum carried him on backward, down the way they'd just climbed, stumbling and flailing, right to the edge…and beyond. His foot went over the side and he tried to turn round or turn aside, but all he succeeded in doing was grabbing at an overhanging jut of rock.

"Jagger?" he cried, clinging on, locking his hands around the spur and trying to swing his dangling legs up onto it. He couldn't. Not once he'd gotten a look at the ground below him…at how far below him it was, where he hung, sticking out over a mountainside on a crag of rock. He banged his eyes shut and looked at the side of the mountain. It wasn't sheer. It was grassy and rocky, with ledges and cracks, bumps and holes. He could work his way to the start of this lump of rock and get his hands and feet to the surface. He could—

He froze, his hands supporting his entire weight.

"Is there...?" Jagger's voice wavered, and Brick risked a peep up to see him standing there, pale. He coughed and his voice worked again. "Any point in me suggesting you shift?"

Brick didn't bother answering.

"Fine. Well, I won't bother telling you to hang on."

Noise suggested Jagger was scrambling down the side of the mountain too. Taking peeps, Brick saw him climbing down lower than where Brick hung like a broken pendulum. "What are you doing?" he yelled.

It was obvious what Jagger was doing, or trying to do—get himself below Brick, onto a ledge of the mountainside that stuck out in a bulge. The mountain wasn't straight or uniform and this shelf put Jagger as far out as Brick and directly under him. Jagger crouched.

"Drop onto me," he instructed Brick. "Go on. Just let yourself fall. It's not far, see, and you'll land on my back. I'll catch you and hold you."

He couldn't. No matter how much he wanted to. Emotions churned in him, all contradictory and mixed and needing an outlet.

A muffled shout came from below him. "Brick, you nearly had me off this ledge!"

How—? Because he'd shifted his tail, and the long, sinewy appendage was flicking back and forth and up and down in his fear and frustration. It was lashing the shelf below him, where Jagger waited, and if it knocked him free, Jagger would tumble down the mountainside too. "Sorry," he muttered, the word inadequate, focusing on staying in his other-form.

"Drop," commanded Jagger again, and Brick could have sworn he couldn't, wasn't able to, but he did, landing on Jagger's crouched body with a whump. It took the elf a few seconds to recover his breath, but when he did, he straightened, Brick clinging to his back and shoulders like a monstrous monkey. Before Brick understood what Jagger intended, and before he could stop him, Jagger found handholds, then footholds, and pulled himself and his passenger up the mountainside to the path.

It seemed to take forever, and Brick felt too scared to breathe, but as soon as Jagger heaved himself and Brick over the edge and onto the pass, Brick sucked in air. He rolled off Jagger and made sure to haul him clear of the side, onto the relative safety of the trail.

"That..." he started but couldn't finish. "Thank you."

"You'd do the same for me," Jagger replied, flopping onto his back too, to lie beside Brick. He raised his head to peer at him. "Wouldn't you? You'd *better*."

Brick grinned. "Yeah, my turn to rescue you again next time."

"*Again?*" Jagger jumped to his feet. "How so?"

"Well, let's see..." Brick started to list all the times he'd saved the day, or the quest. Fine—there weren't that many but...

"What if we turn back?" Jagger said, not looking at Brick. "Don't go to the summit to seek the Horrorcle?"

"Because of that?" Brick demanded, jerking his thumb over his shoulder at the edge of the mountain.

"No. Well, yes, in a way."

"And not seek out the true meaning of the foretelling? But we wanted to know," Brick replied.

"We did," Jagger said, after a pause. "So, upward and onward?"

He didn't sound any more enthusiastic about it than Brick felt. Brick swung an arm around him as he went to pass him and pulled him close. "Thank you," he murmured, wanting to say much more.

"You're...welcome." Jagger didn't move, instead standing close to Brick and staring into his eyes.

Brick was tired of being weighed down with words unsaid.

"Look, I've never had a serious relationship," they both said together, and stopped.

"I thought we'd stopped doing that!" Jagger exclaimed. "Go on?"

"Oh, I..." Brick didn't know what he'd been going to say but knew what he wanted to. "I'm kind of in love with you," he confessed.

He half-expected Jagger to make some joke about *yeah, you got good taste* or *well, in that case, take a number, get in line*, but instead Jagger reached up a hand and ran his thumb over Brick's bottom lip.

"Since that first meeting in the tavern," Jagger said.

"Yes..." Brick was halfway through his answer when he realized it wasn't a question, that Jagger was saying, or admitting— He couldn't catch what Jagger said next, because he whispered it and his face was tucked into the crook of Brick's neck. But as they started walking again, Brick wondered... Had Jagger said, '*I'm sorry*?'

The day darkened about them, the air growing cold. Brick couldn't keep churning it around his brain any longer. He had to ask. "Jagger—?"

"We're here."

It wasn't the summit but flat ground, indicating they'd arrived at the top of the pass. It didn't look inviting. Wisps of cloud hung around as though the mountain had pierced it, and the atmosphere was dank. The trees grew bare and skeletal and heaps of rocks and stone suggested burial mounds and ruined buildings. Night-black birds cawed from on high, then, one by one dived low, to circle them and perch on the roof of a rocky cave across the space that reminded Brick of a village square. The birds were huge.

Jagger had stilled, and Brick turned to him. "What?" he asked. "Sure, it doesn't have the charm of Kevin's crib, but…"

"I've seen it," Jagger said, his voice quiet. "This."

"So, we're at the right place?" Not that there could be much doubt. "Best get this over with, then?" Brick took a step forward.

"No!" Jagger tried to stop him, but Brick had already put a foot onto the flat rock that was like an arena, he suddenly thought.

And as soon as his weight pressed down, the ground shook, then cracked.

Chapter Twenty-Two

"You must have tripped a switch!" Jagger exclaimed.

"I'm sorry!" Brick shouted. "You know what I'm like and what I do!"

"I do." And he loved it, loved Brick and everything about him. He hoped Brick could read that in his eyes, could see it in the slow up-and-down perusal he gave Brick's gorgeous body, could understand what Jagger's lick of his lips meant. He loved Brick for more than his looks, of course, but that was all he was able to convey right now.

If Brick did get it, there was no time for him to reply. Jagger raised his leg, and Brick slid his dagger free of its sheath and hefted it in his hand. He swung himself back to back with Jagger and they revolved in a careful circle, surveying their surroundings. Jagger drew his sword.

"*There!*" Brick called, and Jagger twisted to see a small metal point emerging from the flat stone of the ground, something sharp piercing the ground with an ear-hurting scrape-squeal.

The metal tip looked like the point of a knife or a dagger, but as it rose, it was long. A sword. With an arm attached. Brick nudged him. "I see it," Jagger replied, not taking his eyes from it…from first the skeleton arm, then body, that pulled itself free of its stone grave to settle its sword and shield into place with a loud rattle of bones that made Jagger shudder.

Crrrr-ack. Sc-rrritch.

The noise to the side of him had Jagger glancing that way, to see a second metal point splitting the stone that they stood on.

"That one's got a spear," Brick muttered.

"No shit." Jagger watched it and its skeleton bearer rise, its movements assured and practiced.

"Oh, I'm pretty close to crapping my pants, believe me," Brick confessed. Another noise came from the other side of Jagger. "More so now…"

Now a third skeleton's risen over there too, Jagger finished for Brick. This one was another spear-carrier. One in front, one to the left and one to the right. "Three's not—"

A series of noises cut Jagger off and dragged his attention in front of him again, where a row of metal points was splitting the ground behind the first skeleton. Seconds later these skeleton bodies emerged too, one by one in deadly synchronization, their weapons ready.

"Tell me that's not what I think it is?" Brick begged, his back still to Jagger's and him presumably unable to see what Jagger couldn't take his eyes from.

"You'd better turn around," Jagger told him, sorry to make him do it but glad when Brick stood beside him once again. He pressed close.

The skeleton army stood to attention with a clatter, resting their spear or sword tips on the ground, then moved as one, startingly swift, to drop into half-crouches, like animals.

"What is it? An army of the dead?" Brick wiped his forearm across his sweating forehead.

"*Un*dead," Jagger suggested. *Meaning they can't be killed.*

The rattle was loud, the shriek louder, and both things Brick and Jagger's only warning before the army advanced en masse, moving as one, step by step by step.

"Gods, they're ugly!" Brick said.

Jagger agreed, if ugly meant terrifying, especially the black voids in the skeleton's round eye sockets and triangular nose holes, a match for the polished obsidian of the round shields that they bore aloft. He and Brick took a step back, then another, then, when the arms raised their weapons and howled a war cry, turned and bolted.

"Get to higher ground!" they both said at the same time.

Jagger was slightly quicker than Brick in running up the wide ledge of a large rocky outcrop to get to its top. It was flat, like a platform, and the skeletons swarmed it, hacking and jabbing at them.

"They fight like people!" Brick exclaimed.

"And fall like them," Jagger said, kicking one away before it could get up with them. Another took its place within a second.

He felt sick when he slashed with his blade and chopped the sword arm of another. It fell back with an inhuman shriek and a clatter, and again another took its place. Were more coming out of the ground, even as this battalion fought?

"Jagger!" Brick cried and jerked his head to alert him to something to his right—a skeleton was starting a run up the ledge, to breach their stronghold. It ascended, using the momentum of its run to leap onto their platform, and Jagger threw himself flat so the enemy soldier flew over him and clattered to the ground behind him in a heap of bones.

Another had made it up to where he and Brick fought, and Brick took care of this one, tripping it, pinning its leg down and stomping on the long femur with his other foot. The crunch of broken bone set Jagger's teeth on edge. Brick kicked the skeleton back down to the lower ground, hitting a further two with it on the way.

"Watch it!" Jagger called—another had scrambled up the side and was rushing Brick while he stood bending near the edge.

"On it." Brick bent lower and the skeleton, unable to halt its flight toward him, tumbled over him and off their platform, aided by Brick's foot kicking it on its way.

Jagger heard it shatter on the ground below. He couldn't spare much attention, not when another was slashing for his legs, perhaps trying to hobble him by cutting his hamstrings. It must have fought dirty when it was alive. *More alive.* As if catching his thoughts, it opened its mouth in a broken yellow and gray grin. It wasn't smiling when Jagger jumped over the swing of its blade. No, it looked evil—more evil—at that.

Jagger backed off a little then turned and ran the few paces he needed to get enough thrust to jump from the ground he was on to the higher rockpile next to it. His foe followed him, or attempted to. His jump lacked the momentum necessary to propel his skeleton body from one level to the other and, with legs skittering in midair like an obscene bug, it fell through the gap between ledges and crashed to the stone ground below.

Jagger spared it a glance and watched its skull roll free of its neck. What were these creatures? Who could have animated them? The Horrorcle, he supposed. He cursed when he saw there wasn't space on this plateau for Brick to join him, or for them to fight. Why had he leaped up here, anyway? He scrambled down broken bits of rock to the ground, swinging his sword in one hand and punching with the other to fight off the skeletons who just kept coming and coming.

With a "*Yeaargh!*" Brick leaped down to join him...losing his dagger on the way. Shouting what Jagger supposed was a wyvern curse, he grabbed a shield from a skeleton and used it to bludgeon and smash.

"There's so fucking many!" he gritted between swings and hits. "Got a plan? Any tricks? Bit of magic?"

"Maybe if I had a second to think," Jagger retorted, disarming a tall skeleton and slashing at another. He didn't think them chanting how much they believed in themselves and their quest would do much here, but he was prepared to try.

"I'm *trying* to shift," Brick said, as if Jagger had been demanding it.

"No, I..." He lost his train of thought, trying to make sense of what he was seeing, what the enemy were doing. They'd paused and in a reversal of their synchronized striding forward when they'd first attacked, were now moving backward, all as one unit.

"They're falling back?" Brick asked, his voice hopeful. "Or maybe it's the end of their working day?"

"I don't think they're in a union." Jagger shook his hair out of his eyes to have an unobstructed view of the line of enemy a few feet away.

The day grew suddenly dark and a rusty, grating bird call filled the air, as if those huge dark birds perched on the roof of the cave had blotted out the sun. Then suddenly, it was the nightmare scene Jagger had viewed in his tear-globe. One skeleton detached itself from the line and flew to them. It was the same one Jagger had seen—when it opened its mouth, he recognized its stumpy teeth.

He knew what was going to happen. It would feint that it was going to attack Jagger but turn just enough to plunge its spear into Brick's chest instead. Into his heart.

"*No!*" Jagger yelled.

The skeleton was on them, spear raised, and Jagger, his foreknowledge as heavy as boulders, dropped his sword and grabbed at its arm. As soon as he closed his hands around its bone, cold as freezing as a winter ocean swept over him, numbing him from his toes up and stopping the breath in his lungs and the blood in his veins. The skeleton arm he was clutching vanished from between his hands. It didn't crumble or dissolve, but just disappeared, from one second to the next…as did all the others, leaving him and Brick alone.

Well, leaving Brick alone, because Jagger slumped to the ground, his life force stolen. The last sight he had was of Brick—

"No! No!" Brick's denial rang around the plateau. He dropped to his knees beside Jagger's body. No, beside Jagger, because even though he'd seen that, had felt it, he wouldn't believe it. He laid Jagger down then slapped his face…too hard. "Sorry! But come on, wake up. They've gone now. You…"

Jagger was colder than anything should ever be.

"You…" Brick thumped on Jagger's chest. Were elves' hearts in the same place as wyverns'? He slammed his fist down in several places to make sure, apologizing each time. Tears ran down his face and soaked Jagger's chest. "You *knew*," he muttered, sitting back on his heels. "Knew something was going to happen…to me. I don't know how you did, but you knew. And you stopped it. Let it take you instead of me. You stupid, stupid elf!"

A triumphant cawing noise had his head jerking up to see the row of huge black birds from the cave mouth were hopping toward him over the stony ground. They moved with purpose, their beady eyes glittering.

Brick let out a hoarse laugh. "Yeah right. Sure. Get stuck in, you and your friends. Not!" He scrabbled on the ground and his hand came up with a palmful of stones that he flung at the carrion birds, scattering them in a flurry of feathers and indignant screeches. "Plenty more where that came from," Brick called after them.

He turned back to Jagger. "I saw those off for you," he told him, wondering what the splash of water that landed on him was, until he touched his cheek and found it wet with tears.

Jagger didn't respond, but lay where Brick had arranged him, his glossy dark curls framing his much-too-pale face, his brown eyes closed. He and Jagger had been through so much in their short time together—

every second had been charged and intense…and Brick loved him.

"No." Brick spoke calmly now, as if refuting something he knew to be wrong. "I'm not losing you. Not like this. Not my soul-bonded."

He threw his head back and roared, like wyverns of old in their caverns under the earth. It was as if something charged through him, charging things *in* him, and he bent his face to Jagger's, feeling the tickle of his beard and mustache briefly before he sealed his mouth to his. What was shifting in him? It felt almost like when he'd part-shifted to use his wyvern tongue in his other-form, but this came from deeper within him.

His breath. It streamed up from his soul and poured into Jagger. Brick held Jagger tight, close, and sent his wyvern breath into his mate's body. Jagger twitched. Just a little, but Brick caught it. He pulled away, not because he needed to heave in more air. In fact, his breath still misted from him. He needed to bathe Jagger in it, and that would be easier, would be quicker and Jagger would spend less time in the Realm of the Dead the more skin he had exposed for Brick to breathe on.

He stripped Jagger as swiftly as he could and worked on him, coating every inch of his flesh with his breath. When he reached Jagger's feet, his toes twitched, as though someone were tickling him. So Brick did it again, breathed on his soles, and Jagger jerked that foot away. Brick was staring so hard at that he jumped at the loud, rusty gasp Jagger gave and only looked up in time to see Jagger's chest suck in, then expand.

He coughed and spluttered, as he had in the pool yesterday, and Brick darted to his top half, to lift his head and shoulders off the ground, to aid his respiration. The best sight he'd ever seen was Jagger's eyes, revealed as he opened them wide and stared at Brick. His lips pursed, as if to ask *why*. At least Brick hoped it wasn't *who*, that he had no memory loss.

"Brick." Jagger sat up and looked down at himself. His naked self. He glanced from his clothes, strewn at random on the ground around him, to Brick. "Gods, you're always horny. And people say elves are bad."

"No." Brick tried to make his voice normal and his eyes free of tears. "Elves are wonderful."

"Glad you think so." The hand that Jagger reached to Brick's face, to stroke it, shook a little. "Seeing as you're bonded to one. You…did know?"

"Oh yes." Brick's nod flung the tear from his eye. "*Yes.*"

The second yes wasn't so much an affirmative reply to Jagger's statement as an eager, fervid agreement.

Chapter Twenty-Three

It was as passionate as their kisses, which went on for a long time, until the pair of them eventually broke apart. Jagger used a fingertip to trace the huge grin on Brick's face when Brick eased away. It went from ear to ear, a beam of pure happiness, although Brick had a right to a smugger one, or even a smirk, after what he'd done.

"Are your kisses part of the package too?" Jagger asked. "Because I definitely feel more alive after them." He half-expected to see sparks arcing from his fingertips.

"I…suppose so." Brick sat back on his heels. "I mean, I don't think I was ever that good a kisser."

"Hey." Jagger cupped his cheek. "That's not right. There's been fire whenever we touched, right from the start." *Which should have been a clue.* He became aware of how dank and chilly the day was. "I'd better make myself decent."

"Here. Let me."

Brick stopped Jagger twisting for his clothes, to put them on, and started dressing Jagger himself. He was probably the worst valet Jagger could ever have imagined, clonking him on the head as he attempted to pull on his shirt, and putting his boots on the wrong feet and having to start again. But none of that mattered. Jagger still felt a little weak, and besides, any excuse to get Brick's hands on him was good. He'd bet Brick thought so too—they were seeking out each other's touch.

"When did you know that we were bonded? Because it wasn't just because of the breath, right?" he asked. "Although that is so cool!" The implications struck him. "Your power's healing? No—more than that. *Resurrecting*." Because he was pretty sure he'd been if not *in* the Realm of the Dead, then hovering on its threshold.

He settled himself, his back to a rock, Brick next to him with their legs tangled together and their hands clasping. "What you did—what you can do—how does it work, Brick? Can you do it for everyone?" Jagger wasn't sure how he felt about that. What Brick had done was intimate. The thought of him doing it for others… Was it selfish of Jagger to want it just for himself?

"I don't know." Brick gave a half-shrug. "Wyvern breath is usually something that's used in public, yeah, for gain. Or it doesn't even have to be used, like with my father. People just knowing he possesses storm breath is enough to make him powerful. I think he's only used it twice in his whole life."

And wyvern lives were nice and long, Jagger knew. "Go on?"

"But I've never heard of…what I did. I have a sort of feeling it's one of the things that's only between a bonded pair. They sort of share things. Characteristics. Which I think we have already."

The last sentence came out in a mumbled rush, but Jagger heard it, and understood it...because now he grasped things he thought he'd seen, like their shadows both being wyverns. And things he thought he'd *felt*, like his hand acquiring claws and talons, and his cock becoming— His cock— His breath caught in his chest.

"I'd have to read old Ruby Throne scrolls on it," Brick finished. He tilted his head to get a look at Jagger. "And talking of lore, that's how you knew what was going to happen, isn't it? I remember hearing something about elf tears. I can't recall it all, but it starts 'elves shed no tears in their early years'."

"Really?" Jagger had never heard it put like that. "Finally something that actually rhymes and scans! But yeah." He explained about the tear globe and how it had manifested, and the horrifying scene he'd witnessed in it. "And I couldn't let that happen," he finished.

Brick was silent for a moment. When he spoke, it was with him looking into the distance. "We've been talking about the lore, about the mystical aspect of, well—"

"The *B* word. Bonding." Jagger helped him say it. "Spit it out. Don't be a Kevin about things."

"But not the emotional one," Brick finished.

"Ah." Jagger tightened his hold on Brick's hands. True—he hadn't felt ready to deal with that yet, but he had to. *They* had to.

"You know what it means. It means being together."

The idea of that sent a thrill through Jagger, one that had his lips slanting in a smile.

"You with me and me with you," Brick continued. "Tied. Chained—"

"Angel," Jagger interrupted, the endearment falling from his lips and surprising him as much as it did Brick, going by the startled look on his face.

"*Angel?*" Brick screwed up his mouth as though he were eating citron fruit.

"Because of the wings," Jagger explained.

"Yeah, got that. But still…"

"Prince. That do?"

Brick shrugged, which Jagger took as a yes. He took Brick's face in his hands and spoke with his lips inches from Brick's. "The words you were using. *Tied. Chained.* Interesting language…and activities. Is that something…you're open to trying?"

Brick's eyes opened wide and a dull flush spread across his face. Jagger wouldn't let his prince duck away though. "I got a few ideas I always wanted to try…" Brick muttered, and damn if Jagger didn't get flashes in his mind's eye of what those 'ideas' were. "But it seems cruel."

"Not if it's consensual," Jagger assured him. "And if both parties are aware of—"

"No!" Brick pulled away and got to his feet. "Not that." If he'd attempted to put distance between himself and Jagger, then him bending to help Jagger up too undercut that. "I mean it always felt mean to make someone be with me perhaps against their will. You've seen how I get around magic. How I react. If it's not a nosebleed, it's— Well, worse. I can't remember stuff and get it wrong. I'm dull and plodding and—"

"And I never wanted to settle down with one person. Being with just one person forever? I thought it was a death sentence!" Jagger cut in.

"Oh." Brick gave a nod and half-turned away.

Jagger swung him back. "But that was before I met you. Brick! You're probably the most exciting person

I've ever met. Not just sexually, although there you give me a run for my money and then some."

Brick stood stolid and stoic, like he was waiting for the punchline and that the joke would be on him.

"I love your steadfastness, your stubbornness, that you won't give up. Your curiosity, about people and things and places. Your eagerness to see and try something new. All your knowledge and ideas. Look at all we've done in the course of a few days," Jagger continued. "So just imagine the rest of our lives, because I am."

The smile that turned into a grin on Brick's face was the most wonderful thing Jagger had ever seen, until Brick nodded. That was the best sight ever. "Which makes sense, seeing as we love each other, by the way," Jagger added, waiting for Brick to nod more at that and whisper his agreement.

He didn't know if Brick could see the images playing in his head, all the places they could go, the things they could do there… "And there'd be no problem with your allergy."

"Sensitivity!" Brick broke in. "No, fuck it. *Allergy.*"

"To magic," Jagger plowed on. "Not with you having access to my elven magic, just as I partake in your wyvern ways…" This time he was sure Brick was picking up the images spooling in Jagger's mind's eye. The filthy, delicious images. "There must be something you always wanted to try," he coaxed.

"Well…yes. Maybe," Brick babbled.

"Like?" Jagger pushed.

Brick bent a little to whisper in Jagger's ear, and Jagger's eyes flew wide open.

"Really?" he gasped. "The *tail*?" He peeped over Brick's shoulder at his rear as if expecting to see it. *Wanting* to see it. To experience it.

"Really." Brick nodded.

"Well, *fuck me,*" Jagger breathed.

"That's kind of the idea," Brick looked coy.

"You, my prince, are decadent." Jagger recalled the claws, around his dick. That element of danger. "Debauched." The tongue. *Sweet Mother of Elves, the tongue.* He grabbed Brick to pull him into a kiss. "Depraved," he whispered against Brick's lips.

The creaking sound behind him had him tearing his lips free and whirling around…to see the large rock that had been at the entrance to the Cave of the Worlds was rolling away. "I guess the Horrorcle will see us now?" he said, sounding braver than he felt.

"We don't have to. Like you said." Brick nodded at the cave.

Jagger knew his valiant prince wasn't scared, so waited for him to explain.

"Because what if she says the prophecy isn't about us? That we don't have to make the alliance?"

That we're not bonded, Jagger heard. He settled his sword belt and straightened his leather coat. "Prophecy shmophecy. Who listens to that old bull? No matter what it means, we're together." He'd tell Brick that as often as he needed to hear it, to believe it. "But aren't you curious about who was trying to stop us getting here? Because I really think that's what was happening. Don't you?"

Brick narrowed his eyes, and his forehead creased, as though he were going over everything that had tried to come between them and this place.

"The hobgoblins, the stymph birds, the river, the bounty hunters?"

"Earth. Air. Water. Fire," Brick replied.

Oh. True. "And then, when we managed to get into the forest, and especially when we got deeper, right up until here, more things?"

"But they felt different, somehow," Brick argued.

"Well, I'm tired of being pushed around! Aren't you?" Jagger demanded. Brick nodded. "So let's go ask the question and get this over with."

Hand in hand, they ducked under the low entrance and marched in where Brick let out a muffled scream and pointed. "It's true! You have to face your worst fears!"

Jagger had to admit his own heart thudded at the huge, distorted version of himself in front of him. "So your worst fear is that your butt looks big?"

"My..." Brick whipped around, and Jagger wanted to laugh at the elongated-to-impossible-proportions reflection of Brick in the mirror to their right.

A glass to their left showed Brick's body bent like a circus contortionist. "Oh, I wish I could really do that," he said.

Jagger sort of wished they weren't here, especially when a high-pitched cackle screeched out from up on high. No, over to their left. Wait—behind them. Then, finally...inside his head. He clutched it in his hands and when he looked up, the Horrorcle was there.

"Can you see...her?" he asked Brick.

Brick nodded, staring at the shrouded black figure wreathed in dark-gray smoke.

She hovered, not touching the ground, yet she seemed solid. She didn't seem that frightening. As Jagger thought that, cold dread entered his mind. No, his *soul.* It was just a touch, as if by a tendril or a plume of the smoke surrounding the figure but left him no doubt that it could invade his whole body and seize it, paralyze it. "Sorry," Jagger whispered.

"I know what you seek."

The voice spoke inside his mind, and Jagger glanced at Brick, wondering if he were hearing it too. Brick squeezed his hand *yes.*

"To earn the truth, you must give me a sacrifice."

"What?" Brick asked.

"You two must part ways."

"Really." Jagger had been expecting something like this.

"Only for a few harvests. You will come together again when five winters have passed, with untold riches and power, and your fate is your own."

"Five fucking years apart when we've just found each other?" Brick howled. "No way. Nothing's worth that!"

"Too right. We're not waiting half a decade to marry," Jagger told the apparition, or whatever it was.

"Yeah— Marry?" Brick stared at him. "When did you propose? I must have been asleep and missed it."

"Oh..." Jagger was embarrassed. "Maybe you were belching, and didn't hear me?"

Brick folded his arms across his chest and pouted.

"I like your belches," Jagger assured him. "And I'll get down on my knees properly as soon as we get out of here, okay?"

"Knees? Shouldn't it be knee?" Brick frowned.

"Not for what I have in mind." Jagger winked. "I'll propose as well."

"Marriage?" Brick queried, showing how well he knew Jagger. "And if you do, who's to say I'll accept?"

"Oh, I can be very persuasive." Jagger gave a slow lick of his lips, dropping his gaze, and was rewarded by a groan.

"I am still here!" the Horrorcle hissed indignantly. *"And if you would still seek the truth of the prophecy and*

your quest and those behind both, look no further. If it's not too much trouble, elf."

"You pissed her off," Brick observed.

"*Me?*" Jagger started to argue, stopping at the slithering, wisping sound from farther in the cave.

A veil floated away from something sparkling and gleaming on one wall of the cave, and he found he couldn't resist stepping up to it, drawing Brick with him. A huge mirror.

"So, we're going to learn who's responsible for all we've been through…" He trailed off. He didn't know most of the people he could see forming in the mirror but recognized a family resemblance—to Brick. Some of the people he did know…like his father, Jerrick, and his king, Jade.

"I don't…" Brick started to say, then grabbed wildly for Jagger as they were both sucked through what wasn't a mirror, but a portal…

Chapter Twenty-Four

"Finally!" observed his mother, as he and Jagger landed, the impact crashing them to their hands and knees. She set her cup down on a table and stood, gesturing that he should stand too.

Brick supposed he should. The room's opulence said it was part of the private royal chambers, and if Brick had been in any doubt, the presence of the Storm King and his betrothed would have confirmed it. He rose and bowed, sneaking looks around at his family and the half-dozen elves present. The Ruby Throne was dressed in their ceremonial finery and the elves' sashes and medals—and ages—proclaimed their senior status.

"Jade?" Jagger called across to the king, who was having a crown fitted onto his elaborately braided hair. He pointed to what had been the gaping hole they'd traveled thorough, but was now a small shiny decorative swirl, high on the wall. "Did we just come through a Storm portal?"

The Storm King raised an eyebrow, making the markings he bore between them look skewed. "You know about them?"

"That they're one of the features of the palace that respond only to the ruler? Yes." Jagger laughed, looking younger. "Haven't seen one since I was an elfling, at some party or other, and the Storm Emperor was taking us brats on a tour of the family rooms. He banged his fist on an ornate mosaic tile on the wall and we all got the shock of our lives when the tile lengthened and widened then swung open to reveal a short passage behind it."

"Ahem." Brick elbowed Jagger. "That side trip down Memory Lane's a bit beside the point. We should be asking questions! Like, how?" He jerked his thumb over his shoulder, at the portal, the end of their journey. "Or what?" He indicated the gathering.

"Why?" called Scarlet.

"Or, who?" muttered Jagger, eyeing the room.

"Oh, sorry." Brick cleared his throat, hoping some grand, occasion-appropriate words and gestures would come to him. They didn't. "Jagger, royal-adjacent elf. My family." Shrugging, and ignoring Jagger and Scarlet's sniggers, he made the introductions as quickly as possible.

"Honored and delighted." His mother knew what to say and do, even if she did smell of sweet wine and teeter a little as she curtsied. "To meet my son's soul-bonded."

She took the cup a page handed her and clinked it against the cup of a senior elf who bore a resemblance to Jagger.

"As am I to meet my son's mate-bonded!" he replied, his wine sloshing a little.

They entwined arms and drank. Scarlett whooped. Milly and Gules clapped. His father narrowed his eyes at his wife and the elf.

"You know each other?" Brick gasped, looking from his mother to Jagger's father. He ignored Scarlet's "Duh."

"And we knew you were each other's mates," the elf confirmed.

"And that neither of you would believe it if we just told you!" Cerise added. "You're both so stubborn." She drained her cup. "And besides, it was fun!"

"*Father?*" Jagger gasped, as the elder elf laughed until his eyes streamed. "Oh, yes, Jerrick, Brick."

Jerrick kissed Brick on his forehead, in the spot where an elf mark would be. "Your lady mother and I go way back," he confided.

Brick sank into a chair, leaping up as he remembered he was in the presence of royalty, then sitting again when Jade waved him down. Jagger took the chair next to him. "So this was all a *plot*?" he asked.

"Catch up, bro," Scarlet advised, sliding a goblet down the table to him, and one to Jagger.

Brick sucked in half of the fruit wine in one swallow. "But all that—the goblins, the birds…"

Jagger slapped his hand on the tabletop. "I knew it was all too expensive for Almighty Mallon to hire!"

"My good lady wife called some people. She has a lot of contacts," Carnell told him.

"True, my mother knows everyone," Brick muttered to Jagger.

"Including my father…" Jagger replied.

Brick had been trying not to glance at Cerise giggling with Jerrick, or at Carnell glaring at Jerrick.

"They're old friends. They go way back," said Gules, slinging his arm around his father's shoulders. He was such a peacemaker, even without using his wyvern breath.

"Tell them the rest." Scarlet made a kissy face for an attendant to paint lipstick on her. "That you lost track of them in the Forbidden Forest!"

"Well, we didn't think they'd get that far," protested Jerrick.

"The thinking was you'd turn back when you dropped into the river, and conquered the last of the four elements, who was supposed to meet you *there*," Gules said.

"Elements as in earth, air, water and fire?" Jagger asked, looking at Brick, who'd said that.

"Wyvern thinking." Brick finished his drink.

"Wyvern ways." Jagger grinned.

"Yes, you were supposed to come home then, realizing that you were..." Cerise made a gesture. "But oh no, you're much too stubborn. Oh, and anything after that was all you. You scared us!" she scolded.

Brick stared wide-eyed at Jagger, recalling all they'd been through in the forest, and under the forest, and out of the forest...

"Befriending dryads and humans, forging alliances..." Grlind listed.

"Is all perfect for an ambassador role," Jade finished, Jerrick and Brick's parents nodding. "It's time we sent someone to the human realm."

"My liege." Honored, Jagger bowed.

"Now that you've conquered your fears." Jade waved at Jagger and Brick.

Have we? "You can go in small spaces now," he told Jagger, getting in a preemptive glare at Scarlet in case she ewwwed them.

"And I'm not too scared to share my life with another," Jagger added. "Because that's what a lot of that was."

Oh. All that denial…it made sense. "But I don't know what I won?" Brick said.

"Apart from me?" Jagger grinned. "You're more confident in yourself and your abilities. If you mess up, you try again. And you're not afraid to try."

"When you put it like that…" He had come a long way, and not just physically, through the forest. "The human realm! Think they have moss sandwiches?" Brick asked Jagger.

"And moss soup?" Jagger replied. "And I can meet your kangaroo friend."

Brick thought about how they'd arrived back at the palace. "And I suppose the Horrorcle's another friend of yours, Mother?" he asked her.

"Hardly." Cerise shivered. "But she did owe me a favor, and I called it in when I needed to."

"Ah, true statecraft." Jerrick bowed to Cerise.

"When did you know you were bonded?" Milly asked. Was that a note of longing in her voice? *Well, well.*

"I think…when I could part shift some body parts into wyvern-form," Brick answered, then blushed, more so when Jagger coughed.

"*Ewwww!*" Scarlet cried. "*Much* too much info, bro."

"No, *more* information!" Carnell demanded. "Because that's so extremely rare as to be unheard of! Oh, we have so little research into inter-species bonding. I guess it's because you're accessing Jagger's magic?" He rushed to the elderly councilors, presumably to fill them in, stopping when bells started ringing outside, their peal one of happy triumph.

"The wedding!" Brick had only just realized it must be right now.

"And after—" Jagger started to say.

"We're running away again, before that lot start studying us," Brick finished for him, draining his goblet.

* * * *

The wedding ceremony, as ceremonial and yet heartfelt as it was in the beautiful hall, barely registered with Brick. What his family, and Jagger's father, and his king, had done to him and Jagger was sinking in, making him exchange *can you believe it?* and *the nerve, interfering like that!* glances with Jagger.

"We'd have found each other," Jagger assured him, when they were able to speak, and to do without being overheard. "Oh, the good bit's coming up…"

The king and consort were pronounced bonded, united, one, and invited to kiss to show that to all those witnessing their marriage. Those present who were also in that blessed bonded state were invited to follow suit to demonstrate that too, and Brick squeaked in surprise when Jagger pulled him into an embrace. He sneezed.

"Oh no," muttered his mother. She turned to his father. "I thought you said that Brick would be fine around magic, because of Jagger?"

"I did…" Carnell looked ready to weep.

"My bond-father, bond-mother…" Jagger held up a finger as if to tell them he had it under control. He swept his elaborate hat from his head and cast it to the floor, then pulled Brick to him again. "That damn feather..."

Kissing Jagger without the tip of his plumed hat bothering Brick was much better.

"And now, after—" Jagger started to say.

"It's the celebration fair in the palace grounds!" Sylph shimmered into being at Brick and Jagger's side to announce, making Jagger start violently and attempt to draw his sword. "Oh." Glints and glimmers showed Sylph's hands on its hips. "Handy with his weapon, is he?"

"You have no idea," Brick replied. "So, that's what you were trying to say, Jagger, that there's a fair?"

"No." Jagger scowled, pressing into Brick, making it clear he had a different sort of celebration in mind, and scowling harder when they were swept out into the grounds to rejoice with the rest of the people. "Just you wait until later," he told Brick.

* * * *

As much as Brick ached to be alone with Jagger, being out in public with him, their hands clasped together, thrilled him. "The entire town must be here," he marveled, gaping at the tents and kiosks and booths, at all the revelry and festivities. "Along with all those who came here from their kingdoms to attend. Oh, look!"

"The dragonfly delegation, putting on a display." Jerrick dropped back from where he was walking ahead with the Ruby Throne to tell them. The tiny creatures fluttered in a massive cluster, beating their iridescent wings as one, and changing hue row by row, the effect like a blush sweeping through the group, or a wave breaking over them. They broke apart and came together again in a heart shape, that they turned a deep pink color and made rise then swell growing bigger then smaller, as if it were beating.

One dragonfly was conducting the rest, a tiny baton in his right front leg, and he noticed the wyvern party, bowing to them, then issuing a command to his cluster. Within seconds, the insects had formed the shape of a winged, tailed creature and turned blood red. The wyverns applauded and cheered, and Cerise curtsied at the honor, fake-coughing at her daughters when they didn't follow suit quickly enough.

Next to it stood a pastel-hued tent with its opening pinned back either side. "What's in there?" Brick asked Jagger.

"Love fairies. Don't go peeping in." He tried to block Brick from seeing through the transparent viewing panels.

Brick caught a glimpse of lithe, delicate-looking creatures on chaise longues and divans. "There's gotta be a whole frolic in there!" he exclaimed. "They're getting ready to do something. What?"

"One another," Jagger replied. "Let's move on."

"Why? Is it bad to look?" Then why did they have see-through windows, which people were lining up to peer in?

"No, it just gets me horny," Jagger replied, grinning at Brick.

About to reply that everything got Jagger horny, Brick spied his sister Scarlet making for the tent's opening. "Scarlet!" he yelped, grabbing for her.

"What?" she asked. "One of us has to make contact with the Love fairy king, Artaxis, sound him about forging an alliance with the wyverns."

"So you're taking one for the family?" Brick jammed his hands on his hips.

"Oh, I think she'll be taking more than one…" Jagger whispered in his ear.

"Arrgghh!" Brick glared at him. "I do not want to think about my baby sister in a threesome."

"Threesome?" Scarlet turned back to reply. "That's so last century. It's all foursomes and moresomes now. Don't wait up!"

"Let's go this way." Jagger bore him off. "How good's your aim?"

"For…" Brick studied the game they'd arrived at, which appeared to be a big tank with something reddy-orange and dripping wet throwing itself at the glass and hammering it with its fist. He couldn't hear what it was yelling but doubted they were remarks on how good the weather was for the fair, or how large the crowd.

"Dunking the fire daemon." Jagger flexed his arm and rotated it.

"I've had enough fire and water. What's in there?" Brick stooped to read the wooden sign outside a closed pavilion. '"Wrestle a vicious troll'? Do I have to?"

"No." Jagger grinned. "Is this next tent more your style?" He led Brick to a plastic mat where a woman sat with a box of paints by her side. "I'll treat you. One Grlind, please," he called and pushed Brick forward to have his face turned bright green.

"It's really for kids." The painter lady's forehead creased in confusion. "Adults are using that, there."

That was a life-size picture board of the groom and groom, with holes cut out where their faces should have been, for people to stick their faces in from the back, and make the spectators laugh.

"Oh, he's young at heart," Jagger assured the woman.

"Very funny." Brick tried to elbow the elf in the ribs, but he twisted away, his dark curls dancing. "I'd want to be the Storm King, if anything."

"Jade costumes are over there," the painter lady called up, pointing with a dripping brush.

There were, on the next stall—long black wigs with ear tips sticking out at the sides and strips of black markings to stick on the forehead. *For leisure and entertainment purposes only* announced big labels on each item. An exotic pet stand stood next to that, a trio of mean-faced caterwauls on its counter.

"Ideal for kids!" cried the stall holder, nursing several scratches, his tone desperate.

"Mommy, can I have a chameleon monkey?" begged a small boy.

"You *are* a chameleon monkey," she replied through gritted teeth. "I swear."

It was noisy and crowded and chaotic and Brick, hand-in-hand with Jagger, his bonded, loved it.

"Think this is fun, wait until later." Jagger winked.

Chapter Twenty-Five

"Tell me again why we're out here in the twilight?" Brick asked, looking around the courtyard. "Well, not just us, but…"

"Other bonded couples and…throuples." Jagger had seen some earlier. "Well, it's a privilege."

"I know it's something like witnessing the bedding of the married couple. Which I *so* don't want to do," Brick said. He rubbed his forehead and twisted to peer up. "Storm's coming."

More than he knows, thought Jagger, holding in a smile. Brick had no idea what they were in for, and in truth, neither did Jagger. But he knew it was going to be magnificent.

Thunder rolled, starting high and approaching, and the light changed. At his side, Brick straightened up, feeling as energized as Jagger did, he'd bet. Brick sniffed. *Ozone.* The electric surge of the storm hung in the air, gathering, waiting, and adding to the thick vibe of arousal in the air.

"So we're here for the storm?" Brick tore his gaze from the sky to the foreign royals and diplomats gathered with them in the enclosed square. "Don't they have them, back where they're from?"

"Not like this. There's nothing like a Storm King storm." Jagger took Brick's hand. A current ran between them. Thunder rumbled so loudly that the ground shook. When he'd been younger, a too-close reverberation like that had made him imagine angry sky giants battling each other, but this conveyed two huge beings rolling over and over in a far more intimate and sexual act.

"It's..." Brick lowered his voice, although normal volume was hard to make out over the whistle of the wind. "The consummation of the royal marriage?" He looked toward Jade's tower. Jagger nodded.

The sky darkened to an onyx tinged with jade and it should have looked frightening but didn't. It looked powerful, yes, a potent force, but beautiful as the storm gathered then grew then raged, cloud-to-cloud lightning cracking over their heads. Several fat raindrops struck Jagger's head and shoulders and Brick exclaimed as it became cool rain, misting down on them.

His eyes wide at the wonder of it, Brick pointed up, in case Jagger missed the lightning tendrils flickering silver against the sky. Jagger flung his arms wide to embrace the wave of energy the storm emanated. Lightning struck the ground in front of them, making people cry out and dart away.

"My ears!" Brick covered them with his hands.

Jagger's popped too, and he nudged Brick to be ready...just before the wind whirled down into the courtyard and lifted them and the others there, hovering them above the cobbled ground. Everyone else only managed a few seconds in the air before crashing down again, but they didn't have a wyvern as their bonded, one who shifted in a second.

Brick in wyvern form was magnificent. Jagger didn't think he'd ever not marvel at the tawny beast whose long body and powerful wings were designed for flight and whose lithe neck was twisting to seat Jagger on his ridged back and who asked, in Jagger's head, *"Wanna fly?"*

The heavy storm clouds were no deterrent to Brick. Neither was the lightning striking overhead and about them like massive shards of broken glass, or the deep rumble that shook the earth. Jagger had to make a grab for Brick's ridges and hold on tightly when Brick shook his face, spraying Jagger with the fat raindrops he'd been shaking free of it. The extra shower made Jagger laugh.

Lightning bolts lanced all around them and the deftness and speed with which Brick dodged them took Jagger's breath away. His blood sang and his head spun with the electricity permeating the air. Elves were always told to go in during storms. He could hear his father telling him *"Lightning goes after the highest spot,"* and as he thought that, both he and Brick looked up at the tallest tower.

Brick had to dip with a plummet and roll suddenly to avoid a strike, and Jagger's wet fingers could hardly hold on. But he trusted Brick, knew that if he fell from his seat, Brick would be underneath him, saving him before he hit the ground. Well, he hoped…

They landed on the tower roof and Jagger slid free. Brick didn't immediately change to his other-form, so Jagger touched him, gently, as if reminding him, then had to step away when Brick shifted. Jagger hung back a little, stripping and watching Brick, who hadn't clothed himself, standing on the battlements, his arms out and braced on the stone, his head tilted up to watch the display in the heavens.

It was worth watching, with the night lit up by the lightning spreading out in all directions. It illuminated the strong lines of Brick's body, his wide shoulders and broad chest and taut ass. The air seemed to pulse, the wind knocking into them from the left, rocking them, then striking from the right, buffeting a little harder.

"Like it?" Jagger had to ask.

Brick didn't reply in words, but his slow nod and the awe on his face when he turned it to Jagger answered for him. Jagger came to stand beside him, high above the palace, high above the kingdom to watch the flickering rays of light that seemed poised to set the sky ablaze. Jagger put his hand on top of Brick's where it rested on the crenellated stone and felt the hum in his skin too. They both took deep breaths, filling their lungs with the storm's essence.

The lightning thinned, shooting multicolored trails into the sky like fireworks, and Jagger couldn't wait a heartbeat longer. He eased behind Brick, pressing close and nipping his neck and winding both arms around his sides to caress Brick's bare chest…including one hard nipple and one nipple ring.

"I'd better have the other done," Brick said, his voice unsteady as Jagger fondled him. He tipped his head farther to the side, exposing more skin for Jagger to bite.

"And there," Brick whispered when Jagger's hand traveled south, smoothing down his stomach to his hard cock.

"You don't need to," Jagger assured him. "I love it as it is." To prove it, he eased around, getting between Brick and the balustrade, and dropped to his knees on the stone floor. "Don't mind me. You enjoy the show."

Brick hissed when Jagger grasped the base of his erect cock and closed his lips closed around it. Jagger probed the slit with his tongue, lapping up the first of the salty pre-cum. He kept his eyes on his bonded, watching Brick's golden eyes turn other colors, reflecting the hues streaking across the sky, and how his beautiful lips fell open as he gasped.

"Make sure you don't miss anything, prince," Jagger ordered him. He brought up his other hand to cup and lightly squeeze Brick's balls, wondering if Brick realized he'd widened his stance, to encourage Jagger or if his body had done it for him. "This is a once-in-a-lifetime event."

"Depends on how long…your lifetime is," Brick managed.

Chuckling, Jagger opened his mouth wide and deep-throated Brick, taking him down to the root in one swallow, to suck hard on the still-hardening cock he loved so much. He wanted to do this for him, give him this, to make him feel as good as Brick did him.

Jagger squeezed Brick's balls, teasing the sensitive skin behind them with the tips of two fingers, seeing how quick he could make the wyvern moan and start rocking his hips…and maybe part-shifting his cock, because Jagger was more than curious to feel those wyvern ridges banding it again. But if not, this was more than perfect.

"That's it, prince," Jagger pulled free to say. "Let yourself go."

Brick did. The noises falling from him became groans and his hands relaxed their grip on the battlement to spear into Jagger's hair. He slid his dick through Jagger's lips, thrusting into his mouth to press against the back of his throat. Jagger relaxed his muscles there and loosened his grip on the base of Brick's cock to slide his hand around the cool, rain-misted skin of Brick's side and grip one firm, flexing butt cheek.

"Jagger!" Brick stilled and the tightening of his hands in Jagger's hair stopped him giving Brick head. He reluctantly let that delicious cock pop free of his mouth. Yellow-gold eyes glinted down at him. "Stand up and turn around. I need to fuck you," he added, with an impatient stomp of one bare foot when Jagger wasn't quick enough.

My own fault, Jagger supposed. "I'm just too good at—" Being spun around and bent over the stone wall cut the rest of his smart-assed words off. "Lube. Pocket," he got out, craning his neck at Brick. When he faced front again, the unexpected loud cracks and vivid bursts of colors overhead almost had him falling over the side of the tower.

Brick was soon there once more, a warm, solid presence behind him, stroking a large, strong hand over his cock. He used a foot to make the spread of Jagger's legs wide enough to stand between and got a palm to the small of Jagger's back to angle his body just right to fuck him. Brick's hands were cool when they parted the cheeks of Jagger's ass, and the fingers that swiped up his crack were wet.

"Can't wait," Brick told him, warning him that there wouldn't be much preparation.

Jagger didn't need it, craving Brick deep in him more than he did any foreplay. He gripped the stone posts at the edge of the tower and rubbed his ass into Brick's crotch, his mouth opening on a sigh to feel the blunt push of Brick's cock at his hole.

"Push back. Take me deep," Brick whispered, and the almost shy tone to his request had Jagger's heart melting even as he obeyed, spreading his legs farther and taking Brick's cock into him.

He wanted them to go slow, to savor their joining, but the storm wouldn't allow it. It was reaching its crescendo, the spill of colors that were crackling across the sky and the distant rumbles of thunder making Brick rock his hips hard into Jagger.

He didn't forget his bonded's needs, of course. He reached forward to wrap a hand around Jagger's cock, and the instant overwhelming pleasure he pulled from Jagger made him grip the stone in front of him hard. Brick's cock pushing over that gland deep inside Jagger sent lightning into him, sizzling into his balls. He shouted out to the night when his release shot from the tip of his cock and over Brick's hand.

Behind him, Brick cursed and his hands firming to an iron-hard grip on Jagger's hips had him clamping down on Brick's shaft inside him and trying to stay in position as Brick slammed into him, fast and swift before he yelled as loudly as Jagger had done and his cum filled Jagger.

The entire sky lit up in a flare of pure brilliant white, and there was silence. No sounds from the heavens, or from the masses who must have been below. There was only the galloping of his and Brick's hearts and their broken panting. A second later, the sky gleamed its normal color, although the stars were brighter.

"It's over," Jagger murmured at last, when he could speak. He straightened up with a crick of his back.

"No." Brick slid free and spun him around. "Is it hells—it's only just the start!" He gave a small laugh. "And I thought you were supposed to be the clever one."

"Nah." Jagger teased Brick's spent cock, wondering how soon he could get him hard again. "I'm the dashing one."

"Jagger, Jagger, sword and swagger." Brick looked delighted when Jagger reacted to him repeating the rhyme. "I heard someone say it earlier, at the fair." He looked as though he were about to say something else but laughed instead, almost choking on it.

"What?" Jagger asked.

"The fair. All this..." Brick swept an arm out. "Just for the wedding, right? So I'm wondering what you do around here for anniversaries."

"Oh." Jagger nodded. "Stick around and you'll find out."

"Just you try and get rid of me," Brick replied.

"Nah. Think I'll keep you around. Seeing as we're bonded," Jagger teased. "And besides, I haven't discovered all of your wyvern ways, yet."

"Well, with a bit of elven magic..." Brick came to stand beside him and, arms around each other's waists, Jagger's head in the crook of Brick's neck, they watched the moon rise fat and gleaming in the sky, blessing them and their union.

Want to see more from this author? Here's a taster for you to enjoy!

Intrinsic Values: Artifacts

Bailey Bradford

Excerpt

The *Help Wanted* sign in the window stopped Aldric in his tracks. He'd been walking along San Antonio's Pearl District, somewhat lost in his thoughts and worries, so why he noticed the sign, he couldn't have said.

Maybe because it stood out in the day of internet-everything. All the job boards that he'd scanned and the applications for employment that he'd sent in had been online. That was just how it was done nowadays…except not at the business he'd stopped in front of.

Aldric stared at the sign for a solid minute while trying to calculate his chances of being hired if he went in and applied before going home and changing. Not that he had any fancier clothes. Jeans, T-shirts and one button-up were all that was in his wardrobe.

What are the chances someone else will apply and get hired by the time I go home, shower, shave, change and come back?

Whatever the odds were, his empty stomach didn't want to risk them. Blinking away his musings, Aldric pushed his glasses farther up his nose, then caught himself screwing up his face to re-settle them exactly where they'd been. He attempted to smooth down his hair—being thick, it tended to tousle, even though it wasn't long—and reached for the door handle, which was when he saw the name of the place that was hiring.

Intrinsic Value Antique Shop. At least shop wasn't spelled all funky. It was a silly pet peeve he had, people adding extra letters onto words to make spellings like *shoppe* rather than shop. An antique store might have a better reason than most businesses or services to use an old spelling of the word, and he had no reason to be judgmental of anything—something he needed to keep in mind.

Even though he knew nothing about antiques, Aldric opened the door and stepped inside to the tinkling of chimes. He glanced down at the door handle inside and saw strings of silver and copper bells dangling from it.

"Good afternoon. May I help you?"

Aldric pivoted so quickly that he almost tripped over his own feet—nothing unusual for him. Heat rushed to his face, and he gulped as he spotted the older man standing with one hand on an ancient-looking cash register. "Er, yes, I, um, I—" Aldric took a deep breath and exhaled to the count of ten. If he didn't get himself calmed down, he'd stumble over his words as well as his feet, as he tended to do when he was flustered.

"My name is Elliot Douglas. I'm the owner of Intrinsic Value. Please call me Elliot." Elliot came around the counter and stopped in front of Aldric.

"Aldric Beamer." Aldric offered his right hand to shake. "Nice to meet you, Elliot." His mouth was dry, and a tickle started up in his throat.

"Nice to meet you, too." Elliot pumped his hand one more time, then let go. "Are you here about the job? I noticed you standing outside and thought you might be considering it."

Aldric covered his mouth and turned his head before he coughed. He lowered his hand and faced Elliot again. "Sorry, the mountain cedar is kicking my allergies into high gear. Yes, sir, I'm here about the job. Surprised me to see an actual sign in the window. Everything's done online, it seems. I've been told to go home and apply online so often, I've quit thinking about actual signs."

"Ah yes, the internet is an amazing tool for many things, but I prefer to meet people in person first, rather than online." Elliot smiled, and Aldric realized the older, taller man, with his tawny-brown eyes and thick mane of slightly long, wavy light-brown hair that was just starting to silver, was quite handsome.

"Why don't you come back this way and tell me what makes you think you'll be a good fit at Intrinsic Value?" Elliot gestured in the direction of the cash register. "I was cleaning off my baby and would like to finish as we talk."

"Yes, sir." Aldric coughed again and wanted to melt into the floorboards.

"Would you like some cold water or hot tea?" Elliot offered. "I have both available."

Aldric wasn't sure about hot tea. He'd only ever had Texas tea—cold, with lots of sugar and ice in it. But maybe tea was a thing with Elliot. "Er, tea, please?"

Elliot glanced back at him. "You sound uncertain. Have you tried hot tea before?"

Lying wasn't something Aldric did if he could help it. "I haven't, but I thought a warm drink might help with my scratchy throat."

"That it might. I have a few different kinds, but how about you try the chamomile? It's good for all sorts of ailments." Elliot stopped by an elegant-legged wooden table that had a silver tea kettle and several mismatched cups and saucers sitting on it.

A white ceramic dish held glass jars of tea and cubes of sugar, and a clear container was filled with what appeared to be honey. Delicate silver spoons were laid out as well. Aldric tucked his hands into the front pockets of his jeans. Everything on that table looked delicate, not only the spoons, and he was afraid to touch anything.

Which had to mean he shouldn't apply for the job.

"Aldric?" Elliot arched one thick eyebrow. "Is chamomile okay?"

Realizing he'd more than likely made sure he wouldn't get hired, because Elliot had to think he was on the dense side, Aldric shook his head. "It's okay, thank you. I'll just—" He started to take a step back.

"Just what?" Elliot asked, scooping tea from a jar before he put it into a little oval-shaped strainer. "Are you not interested in the job after all?"

Aldric bit his bottom lip and pondered whether he should stay or not. For one thing, he'd already made some kind of impression, good or bad. For another, Elliot hadn't run him off. *That has to mean I still have a chance, right? Until I tell him I know nothing about what this shop sells. Damn it.*

"I'm interested, but I don't have any experience with antiques," Aldric rushed out, watching Elliot pour hot water over the strainer holding the tea. Elliot had put a lid on it so the tea leaves didn't flow out.

Aldric took a step closer, unable to resist getting a better look at what Elliot was doing. He took off his round-framed glasses, polished them and shoved them back on.

"The tea needs to steep for a few minutes," Elliot explained. "The infuser keeps most of the bits of tea leaves from escaping, but you still might have a few pieces in your cup. Those will usually settle at the bottom."

"That's the infuser?" Aldric asked when Elliot nudged the strainer holding the tea.

Elliot smiled at him. "Yes, it is. Do you like honey?"

"I—" Aldric's stomach picked that moment to let out a rumbling growl. He dropped his gaze and pressed a fist to his belly. "Sorry. Skipped breakfast."

"Well, that won't do. It's almost time for dinner. I'll order us something to eat, then you and I will sit down for a proper interview—if you're interested in the job?" Elliot picked up the jar of honey.

"Oh, I…I am, I just thought I'd blown any chance I had at it." Aldric ducked his head and stared at the worn toes of his tennis shoes. "I don't have any experience for it. I've only worked at fast-food places. I don't know anything about antiques. I didn't even know what that thing—the infuser—was." His ignorance was embarrassing, and he hated that he didn't know more.

"So," Elliot drawled, one corner of his mouth curving up. "No experience at all? That would mean I'd have a clean slate in you, if I were to hire you. Wouldn't have to rid you of bad habits and misinformation."

Aldric was almost too afraid to believe he might have a chance of keeping his shitty apartment and not going hungry for much longer, after all. "Are you serious?"

"Utterly. Here, let me fix your tea, then I'll order something from the restaurant across the street. It has a little of everything. I have a menu for it behind the counter. This won't take a moment..." Elliot took the infuser out, then added honey to the tea.

"Thank you." Aldric should have refused the offer of a meal, but the truth was, he was too hungry to let pride cost him sustenance. He took the warm cup of tea from Elliot and inhaled the fragrant steam rising from it. "Oh! This smells good."

Elliot smiled at him, a delighted expression, if Aldric wasn't reading him wrong. "I hope you'll like the way it tastes as well. Let me grab that menu, then you can peruse it with me."

"Okay, thanks." Aldric took a sip of the tea. It was hotter on his tongue than he'd expected, and he winced as he swallowed. He was glad Elliot hadn't seen him do that. The next sip he took was slower. The taste was as pleasant as the smell of the tea, the honey sweet but not overpowering.

"Here we go. I haven't had anything bad from here yet, but then again, I always order the same thing. I'm a creature of habit in many ways." Elliot's smile had turned rueful.

"What do you get?" Aldric asked before taking another drink. He could get addicted to hot tea.

"Nothing adventurous, just the grilled salmon with steamed vegetables and mashed sweet potatoes." Elliot handed him the menu. "I think the burgers should be good, though. Whenever I'm in the restaurant and see and smell them, they remind me very much of the ones my brother used to love."

"Younger or older brother?" Aldric flipped the paper menu open to scan the selections.

Elliot froze for a second, as though something were wrong. Before Aldric could ask him if he was okay, Elliot drew in a breath, then touched his temples, where he had a few strands of gray. "Younger. Chris is thirty-two, Natty is thirty-four and I'm the old man at forty-something. Do you have any siblings?"

Aldric decided he'd get the bacon burger and sweet potato fries. He'd never had the latter before. "I have two, like you. Twins. They're almost twenty years older than me."

Elliot's eyes widened. "That's two whole decades!"

"Yeah. I was a surprise," Aldric muttered. That was a nicer description than his family had called him at times. "Gregory and Simon are forty. I'm twenty-one." He hoped Elliot wouldn't ask any more questions about them, or Aldric's family, period. Hoping to avert such possibilities, Aldric tapped the menu. "Can I get this? The bacon-mushroom burger?"

"Of course, of course." Elliot moved back behind the counter and picked up something black. He stuck one finger in a silver ring that had smaller holes in it, and it took Aldric a moment to realize Elliot was using some kind of old phone.

Aldric had vague memories of his parents having a landline, but by the time he'd been old enough to care about it, they'd had cell phones. Even so, none of the phones Aldric had ever seen had looked like the one Elliot was now speaking into.

Elliot grinned as if he knew what Aldric was thinking, making Aldric look away and take another drink of his tea. When Elliot had looked at him then, it had occurred to Aldric that his potential boss was not only quite handsome, but very attractive. *He's about the same age as my brothers, so gross.* Aldric needed a job more than he needed to get laid, and he'd never been attracted to older men, either—and he wasn't about to start down that road now.

Not that Elliot would be interested in someone like him. Even though he'd only spent fifteen minutes in

Elliot's presence, Aldric could already tell that the guy was much classier than he'd ever be. There was also the very real possibility that Elliot wasn't gay, despite the vibes Aldric was reading. Well, it didn't matter one way or another.

Elliot hung up and tapped the black phone. "It's an ancient rotary phone. My grandparents and parents had these, way back when, although we'd upgraded to a push-button phone by the time I started school. Want to see how it works?"

Aldric was itching to do just that. "Yeah, I mean, yes, I'd like that."

The lesson taught him more than how to dial out on the phone—it taught him that Elliot was a patient and kind man. He encouraged and answered any questions Aldric had, which was freeing in a way that Aldric hadn't experienced before. The old saying about children being seen but not heard had been a rule in his parents' home.

"You have an inquisitive nature and a good brain." Elliot propped a hip against the counter. "I think you'll do well here."

Aldric blinked in surprise. He was glad he'd set the teacup down, or else he might have dropped it, considering how much his hands trembled. "I have the job?"

Elliot nodded. "You do."

"But...what about references and work history?" Aldric regretted asking as soon as the words were spoken.

"I like to believe I have excellent judgment when it comes to people," Elliot said. "Am I wrong in regard to you?"

Aldric shook his head. "No. It's just, I don't know anything about antiques, or what I'll be doing."

"You can learn. Someone gave me a chance a few years ago and made this"—Elliot swept a hand toward the antiques in the shop—"possible. I'm still learning, one might say. That's one reason I keep alphabetized cards on every item in the store, as well as those in the back. If someone asks about, say, this…" Elliot walked over to the second row of shelves and pointed to a silver tray. "What does it look like to you?"

Sweat broke out on Aldric's brow. He knew what the object looked like to *him*, and it seemed obvious—was Elliot trying to trick him? No, Elliot had been nothing but kind to him. Aldric couldn't let his own insecurity get the better of him now. "A-a silver tray?"

Elliot's smile could have lit up the room. "Yes! So you'd just open the gold-leafed book under the register—go ahead and find it. Open it and look up 'silver tray'."

Aldric did as directed and was delighted to discover that most of the cards also had a small image of the item on the right corner. "It's an eighteenth-century silver salver." He read off the rest of the information, relief coursing through him even as he stumbled over some of the words. He could do this job.

"You won't be alone in the store often, not at first," Elliot said. "I'll be out on the floor with you or, once you've been here for a while, in my office. Sometimes I'm away for a day or so, for instance at a fair or auction, or I might have to leave the city, to procure or sell an antique or attend an event, but I close the shop then."

Aldric's excitement fizzled out. "Oh. How…how long would you be gone? How often does that happen?" He'd lose out on work, and if he couldn't support himself—

"I'd have you come in and work in the back while I'm gone. There will always be plenty of cleaning that can be done. I'll show you how to polish silver and clean antiques—the ones that should be cleaned," Elliot added before the door opened, and a young woman carrying a box entered. "Meredith! You are an angel of mercy."

Meredith shook her head, making her brown hair ruffle over her shoulders, and chuckled. "Hardly. I'm just the delivery chick from across the street. Who's this?"

"Aldric Beamer, my new employee," Elliot answered, glancing at Aldric. "Right?"

"He's not sure?" Meredith asked before Aldric could answer. She winked at him. "You should work for Mr. Douglas. He's cool, and I bet he pays well, judging by the tips he gives me."

Aldric hadn't even thought to ask what his wages would be. The whole job-thing had happened so fast it felt like a dream.

"We haven't discussed his pay." Elliot took out his wallet and removed several bills from it. "But, of course, I believe in paying a livable wage."

Aldric knew first-hand that minimum wage wasn't a livable wage. He'd worked just under full-time and had often skipped meals to make rent. More than once, his electricity had been cut off. No fast-food joint he'd worked at had wanted to employ him full-time—that would have meant offering him health insurance. Then things had taken a turn for the worse and he'd found himself unemployed and hovering at the edge of homelessness.

"Aldric?"

Aldric lifted his glasses with one hand and rubbed a knuckle of the other into his eye. "Sorry. I sort of drifted off. I promise I won't do that while I'm on the clock."

Elliot held out a box and a drink. "I have utter faith in your ability to work well. Here, take this and head to the back. Second door on the left is my office. We'll dine in there."

"Fancy," Meredith said, her brown eyes alive with humor. "Nice meeting you, Aldric."

"Nice meeting you, too," he replied, his face heating because he'd mentally checked out in front of her and Elliot.

He found Elliot's office and was almost afraid to sit down in the plush leather chairs. The whole room looked like something out of an old-time movie, with its shiny wood surfaces, smooth leather seats and framed black-and-white photos from decades ago on the walls.

"Have a seat. Well, scoot closer to the desk if you want to use it for a table." Elliot came around to the other side of his desk and sat, placing his own food on it. "There's a coaster for your drink in the wood tray to your left."

Aldric found the coaster and set his drink and boxed meal down before moving one of the leather chairs closer. "This is a very nice office. Is everything in it antique?"

Elliot began removing his food from the box it had come in. "Yes, except the pens and paper. Although I do have a quill pen!" He pointed at a long white feather. "It's not quite an antique, but I like it."

Aldric took a bite of his burger, and his stomach gave a happy rumble. "This is good," he muttered after he'd swallowed.

Elliot grinned. "I'm glad you like it. My salmon smells amazing, as always. Before I start in on it, though, I want to cover salary, hours and health insurance."

Aldric almost choked on the sweet potato fry he'd just bitten into. "Health insurance?" *No.* His ears were playing tricks on him.

But they weren't. Elliot explained how he'd make sure Aldric was covered, without a waiting period. Aldric would have a full forty hours a week, would be paid at time and a half for any hours over that, and while he wouldn't get rich working at Intrinsic Value, he'd earn that much-longed-for livable wage. It seemed too good to be true, and Aldric quickly and gratefully accepted everything he was offered, hoping that nothing happened to make this dream-come-true come crashing down around him.

PRIDE
PUBLISHING

About the Author

A native Texan, Bailey spends her days spinning stories around in her head, which has contributed to more than one incident of tripping over her own feet. Evenings are reserved for pounding away at the keyboard, as are early morning hours. Sleep? Doesn't happen much. Writing is too much fun, and there are too many characters bouncing about, tapping on Bailey's brain demanding to be let out.

Caffeine and chocolate are permanent fixtures in Bailey's office and are never far from hand at any given time. Removing either of those necessities from Bailey's presence can result in what is known as A Very, Very Scary Bailey and is not advised under any circumstances.

Bailey loves to hear from readers. You can find her contact information, website details and author profile page at https://www.pride-publishing.com

www.ingramcontent.com/pod-product-compliance
Lightning Source LLC
Chambersburg PA
CBHW050740180626
46814CB00002B/839

9781839439841